Disappearing Act

By SID FLEISCHMAN

SID FLEISCHMAN

ILLUSTRATIONS BY CHAD BECKERMAN

GREENWILLOW BOOKS
An Imprint of HarperCollins*Publishers*

Disappearing Act

Text copyright © 2003 by Sid Fleischman, Inc.

Title page and dedication page art copyright © 2003 by Jane Wattenberg

Illustrations copyright © 2003 by Chad W. Beckerman
For information address HarperCollins Children's Books, a division of HarperCollins Publishers, 1350 Avenue of the Americas, New York, NY 10019.

www.harperchildrens.com

The text of this book is set in Adobe Caslon.

Book design by Chad W. Beckerman

Library of Congress Cataloging-in-Publication Data

Fleischman, Sid, (date)

   Disappearing act / by Sid Fleischman.

       p.   cm.

   "Greenwillow Books."

   Summary: After their archaeologist mother fails to return from Mexico and they discover that someone is stalking their Albuquerque house, twelve-year-old Kevin and his opera-singing older sister flee to Venice, California, where they hope that new identities will keep them safe.

   ISBN 0-06-051962-2 (trade). ISBN 0-06-051963-0 (lib. bdg.)

   [1. Brothers and sisters—Fiction. 2. Stalking—Fiction. 3. Beaches—Fiction. 4. Opera—Fiction. 5. Orphans—Fiction. 6. Venice (Los Angeles, Calif.)—Fiction.] I. Title. PZ7.F5992 Di 2003 [Fic]—dc21 2002023163

10 9 8 7 6 5 4 3 2 1

First Edition

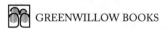 GREENWILLOW BOOKS

FOR
BOB GOLDFARB,
OLD FRIEND

CONTENTS

THE TOAD

1

Hear that screaming? That's my sister, Holly. It's not exactly screaming. It's singing. She's practicing to be a world-famous opera singer. She thinks people will actually pay to listen to her.

I have to listen because she's driving. We're heading for California in her old VW with about a million miles on it. The only thing holding it together is the green paint. Holly couldn't find Los Angeles without me, Kevin. She gets lost going around the block. Aside from her sense of direction, she's brilliant.

We have to get out of New Mexico. Some guy is stalking her. Us, I mean. My picture was inside her purse when he burgled it three weeks ago, and now he is beginning to stalk me, too. He was sending drawings of skulls with my name under them.

The minute school was out, we packed a few things, locked up our house, and just walked away from our friends and everything. We couldn't expect the police to station a cop on our front porch day and night.

Holly keeps looking in the rearview mirror to make sure that the stalker's car isn't following. We don't know what the creep drives or looks like. We call him the Horned Toad. The Toad, for short.

By the time we reach Phoenix we begin to relax and she sings into the wind, some bullfight stuff from *Carmen*. She snaps her fingers like castanets.

I'd help drive, but she won't let me, except when the road is out in the middle of nowhere. I'm twelve, plus, plus. Holly is twenty-one, plus. We both have green eyes and straight brown hair, though mine is longer than hers. She tells me I look like a yak. She's kind of tall for a girl, and I answer back that she looks like a giraffe with earrings.

We may be orphans. Maybe not. I am trying not to think about it.

We reach the Pacific Ocean around eleven at night and park under a streetlight. We splash right in the waves, jeans and all. I've never laid eyes on the ocean in my life, and now it's running down my neck. The thought makes me giggle. Holly, too.

That's the way we stand in the lobby of the motel to register—soaking wet. And ready to start living all over again with fancy new names. She signs us in as Smiths. Smith! Sometimes I think that Holly has no more imagination than a turnip. I'd have called ourselves the Draculas or Svengalis or something to really confound the Toad. Not that he could have a clue that we have washed up in Venice, California.

We sleep for twenty-four hours or so and then find a room to rent. It's in an old beach house all buttered yellow by the sun. It looks friendly. It isn't home with a room of my own, but it will do.

The patio is walled in with blue Mexican tiles and actually has an avocado tree growing in the middle of it. With actual avocados hanging on it. Red flowers climb over the roof like a prairie fire. If that house could talk, I think it would speak Spanish. It's called Casa de Sueños. Holly, who knows everything, says that means House of Dreams. She's good at languages.

Exactly what we need, I think. Dreams. We've had it with nightmares.

THE GARBAGE JUGGLER

2

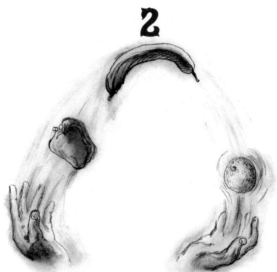

I'd made so much noise about calling ourselves Smith that Holly changed our name to Gomez when she paid the rent.

"Gomez," I whispered. "Do we look Mexican? Who do you think that's going to fool? Whom, I mean."

"The Toad," she murmured.

I gave her a quick grin. The stalker would never think to look for a couple of Gomezes. I felt safer already.

We could hear someone upstairs tap dancing. At the foot of the stairs we had to pass a big, sweaty guy with a short red beard. He was practicing juggling apples and bananas, grabbing bites off the flying fruit as fast as he could. It seemed like a messy way to eat lunch.

"Welcome to the House of Broken Dreams," he said, bits of apple shooting out of his mouth. "You come out here to bust into the movies like everyone else? You ready for your close-ups? You got that wannabe look. Where you immigrants from?"

Ever since the Toad had turned up in our lives, Holly had stopped talking to strangers. I figured as long as our name was now Gomez, it didn't matter what I said. So I gave him our new name and said, "We're from Mexico City."

"Never heard of it," he answered. "Either of you wannabes wanna job? My hat man quit."

Hat man? They must speak their own lingo in California. We started up the stairs with our suitcases, but he kept talking, his mouth spraying bits of apple like sawdust. "Hey—what do you think of the act? I'm the only artiste on the boardwalk who juggles watermelons. Lady Gomez, you want the job?"

We left him standing there snatching his lunch out of midair, and found our room. It had two beds and old movie posters on the walls, one of them of *The Hunchback of Notre Dame*. Wasn't it going to be pleasant at night looking at that creature with the bad teeth bent over my bed? The big, open window looked out on a lot of sand and seagulls. Holly listened for a moment.

"That bird is hitting high C," she said.

"That's a good sign, isn't it?"

"I wonder who its teacher is? I'm going to have to find a new one."

I was glad to see her smiling again. The stalker just about ruined her sense of humor. It didn't do mine any good, either.

We unpacked, which took about twenty seconds. All we had brought along were some extra clothes, my baseball mitt, our mom's dig notebook (she was an archaeologist), and some chit-chatty language tapes. Holly needed to study Italian and French for opera. Books and stuff we left in the car.

Finally she said, "You hungry? Let's eat."

"I'm starving," said I.

"You got any money left?"

"Don't you?"

"Let me have a look."

Holly wasn't very good at keeping track of pesky things like money. She had forgotten to empty her bank account before we left Albuquerque. I think screeching those high notes must rattle the skull at times. Actually I like her voice. I just don't go around humming those weird songs she sings. There's not a bongo drum or electric guitar in any of them.

I asked, "Did we blow everything on rent?"

"It's a roof over our heads, Kevin."

"We could have slept on the beach," I protested. "Maybe we can get a refund."

She shook her purse upside down. A dollar bill and some change tumbled out with her hot red lipstick and a yellow Kleenex and car keys. She didn't carry credit cards anymore, not since the Toad broke into our place and walked off with a lot of stuff. He had the purse with her credit cards and address book, and he even took a lot of letters from our mom that Holly was saving. Who would want to read our mail? The Toad was definitely weird.

He began charging stuff, of course, so Holly canceled all her plastic. Most of the time she stopped wearing lipstick, as if she were trying to turn herself invisible. We left a trail that was strictly cash. Not even a pack of bloodhounds could lead him to us now.

I counted my pocket money and looked up. "Eighteen dollars and forty-three cents."

"It's good to have a rich relative," she said, tying an orange scarf around her hair.

"Can't you call the bank and tell them to send money?"

"And take a chance that the Toad will pick up on it? No, thanks. I'll find a job."

I shrugged. "How about that juggler downstairs? He says his hat quit."

"Do I look like a hat?" she said, striking a pose out of grand opera. "That doesn't sound like a good career move for me."

The guy with the red beard was no longer juggling at the bottom of the stairs. He'd even cleaned up the garbage on the floor.

A skinny man working with a laptop in the patio gave us a welcoming grunt as we passed. He said his name was T. Tex Rimbo and that he was writing a screenplay. It was about potato bugs that take over the world.

"I thought they already had," Holly muttered under her breath.

Finding lunch along the beach was easy. The cement boardwalk was crowded tight with ramshackle taco joints and henna tattoo parlors and hamburger stands and tarot card readers under beach umbrellas.

We ate Mexican, maybe to convince ourselves that our name really was Gomez. We dined like the natives, standing up, and watched the Saturday crowds saunter-ing by, thick as schools of fish. Almost everyone wore shorts or Levis and looked as if they came from some-where else, like us.

The more I thought about it, the more I liked the idea of being able to call ourselves anything we wanted. Not that there was something wrong with the name I was born with, Kevin Michael Kidd, but I hadn't been consulted. Me, Gomez. I kind of liked the sound of it and began to wonder what I should use for a first name. Jose? Diego? Maybe something out of left field. Wolfgang? Englebert? You ought to get a medal for wearing a name like that.

As we wandered along the boardwalk, Holly found a job in about a minute and a half. She saw a sign that said HELP WANTED. The suntanned guy running the jewelry stall was so sweaty, he looked dipped in bacon fat. He checked her feet and said sure, you're hired, kid.

He gave her silver rings to slip on her toes. All she had to do was sit on a high stool under a sign that said

TOE RINGS and show off her foot jewelry to the passing tourists. She didn't exactly stop traffic, and it wasn't the Metropolitan Opera House in New York, but it was seven dollars an hour.

I continued along the boardwalk alone and wasn't too surprised to spy out the garbage juggler. He had an open spot between a fire-eater and a lady who'd write your name on a grain of rice for ten dollars. "Sir," I said. "What's a hat man?"

He began to juggle three eggplants. "Watch this. Stand there, pal, and shill until I get a tip."

What was he talking about?

"Isn't English your native language?" he asked, grinning wide through his short red whiskers. They stood out on his face like iron filings. "A tip, me lad, is a crowd, which I lack at the moment. A shill is someone to stand there and look fascinated. That helps attract the tip. The hat man passes the hat. Got all that? What happened to the lady?"

"She has a job. I could be a hat man. What does it pay?"

"Greedy little wetback, ain't you?"

I looked at him. This was just like New Mexico. "I guess I don't want the job," I said. I was surprised that I felt insulted, and began to move on. Maybe it wasn't such a good idea to take the name Gomez.

"Hold on, buddy. I only tease people I like. You can needle me back. But I've got to tell you, you look about as Mexican as Yorkshire pudding. Let me hear you speak it."

"Speak what?"

"Your native language, Gomez."

I felt a gulp of panic, but then, in the nick of time, a brilliant backhand came to me. "In my home, we only spoke the original Latin."

Without missing a beat, he fired back, *"Fictio cedit veritati."*

Naturally, my jaw came unhinged. Who was I trying to fool? Of all the strange creatures on the boardwalk, I had to tangle with a garbage juggler who actually spoke Latin. California was a wonder.

"Fiction yields to the truth," he said, translating for me. "Now that we understand each other, let's cut a deal. I'll give you five percent of the hat. And that'll make us partners."

I figured he was trying to cheat me, out of habit. If I collected a hundred dollars in his hat, I didn't need a calculator to figure out I'd get only five dollars.

"Ten percent," I said.

He dropped the eggplants, on purpose, I think. "Lord o' mercy!" he exclaimed, and then gave a muscle-bound shrug. "Okay, ten percent."

"How much is that in dollars?"

"Depends on how well you work the crowd, Gomez. Can you smile?"

"Of course."

"Let's see."

"Not until I get paid," I said.

He seemed willing to tolerate me, Latin or not, smiling or not. "Use that lard can with the dollar bills sticking up. Those bills let the marks see we don't work for parking-meter money. And wait until I finish with the watermelons before you start your employment. What'll I call you? Gomez? Luis? Jose?"

"Pepe," I said, to my own surprise. Pepe? That was the name of a friend I left behind in Albuquerque. Well, he wouldn't miss it.

"Okay, Pep, let's go to work."

I kind of smiled to myself. Pep. I liked it. That's who I'd be. Pep Gomez.

"PEP GOMEZ, YOU'RE A GENIUS!"

3

The juggler had a voice loud enough to rattle windows. "Wait! Stop! Watch!" he called out, the shoulder muscles under his shirt rolling as if he had an anaconda under there. "Watch Bumpy Rhoades, the Juggling Jester. The Mighty Muscle Beach Bowwow. Step right up to the World's Only Watermelon Juggler."

He'd begin by taking bites of small fruits, apples and bananas, until the tip—the crowd—was big enough. Then he'd heave three twenty-pound striped watermelons in the air for a finish, and I'd pass the lard can.

In my spare time I couldn't helping staring at the woman dressed as the Statue of Liberty standing across the way. Her face was painted silver, her gown was silver, and she held a torch high up in her right hand. She never moved a muscle. I kept trying to catch her blinking her eyes, but she seemed to know I was watching and wouldn't let me catch her at it.

"That's a mannequin act," Bumpy told me.

"Doesn't her right arm get tired, holding up that torch for hours?"

Bumpy just smiled. It took me awhile to catch on. That was a fake arm on her shoulder. Her real right arm was hidden under all the drapes she wore.

I was beginning to like the boardwalk. I liked becoming part of all the splashy signs, the buzz of voices, and the strangeness.

By the end of the afternoon I had collected an amazing hundred and seventy dollars for Bumpy. He explained to me that if he just put the can on the ground, townies—the local people—slipped away without tossing much in. A hat man working the crowd could double the take. He told me to call him Bumpy and paid me more than my share, twenty dollars even, and I skipped off.

I was feeling pretty good with fresh money in my pocket. I slipped through the boardwalk crowd as if I belonged there. When I found the toe-ring booth, Holly was gone.

It gave me a little start. I felt attached to Holly in a way that I never did when our mom was around. I didn't remember my dad at all; he'd been a flier with the Navy and crashed at North Island, across the bay from San Diego. Holly kept me from feeling like an orphan, and it made me nervous when I lost sight of her.

I tapped her boss's sweaty arm. "What happened to my sister? You fire her?"

"She quit. She said the job was beneath her. Go figure."

I found her in the patio, under the avocado tree, reading want ads in the paper and vocalizing. Singing scales. That's about as much fun as walking up and down stairs.

"Hello, Gomez," she said.

"Pep," I said. "Why didn't you tell me where you'd be?"

"I couldn't find you."

"I was just down the boardwalk. I'll buy you a compass."

"Pep, huh?" she murmured, looking me over as if to grade me on my name change. "Okay."

"I made twenty bucks," I said victoriously. She was impressed. I flopped into a chair beside her, and she went back to running the scales again. After a while, she took out her stopwatch and held her breath.

"A minute twenty-three seconds," she announced finally, pleased with herself. She's aiming for two minutes the way the big-time sopranos can. She runs and stretches like an athlete. She says it's all to increase the muscles behind her diaphragm and all that other inside stuff she needs to sing and not run out of breath.

Upstairs, the tap dancer was still tap dancing. T. Tex Rimbo hung around the patio typing away on his screenplay about giant potato bugs. The place seemed to be a theatrical roominghouse, full of showbiz people. There was even a full-length mirror near the door so you could check yourself before stepping onstage—that is, outside.

Our landlady was showbiz, too. She was a plump movie star named Miss Fiesta Foote.

Not a star, exactly, we discovered. A movie extra. "I specialize in crowd scenes," she said, laughing. She had a nice laugh. There was an upright piano in the living room, and sometimes I heard her bang away at it. But all I ever heard her play were tangos. She'd once been in a movie about Argentina.

Toward the end of the week she told us she was getting complaints from T. Tex Rimbo about the noise from our room. He was finding it hard to concentrate on his potato-bug movie.

In the sweetest voice possible, she said she had to draw the line at renting to sopranos. "Tap dancers and bongo drummers are bad enough, darlings, but nobody wants to live next door to a soprano. You screech."

So we'd have to find another place to live, for I knew you couldn't keep Holly from twittering, even if you put rivets through her lips. I woke up in the middle of the night, hitting my forehead with my hand. I knew what to do.

Pep Gomez, I thought. You're a genius.

FLYPAPER

4

The next day we went into show business under a tall palm tree on the boardwalk. I scared up an empty coffee can, quit my job with Bumpy Rhoades, and Holly began to sing. In faded Levis with holes in the knees. She went into something she said was the "Bell Song" from *Lakmé*.

It had more high notes in it than a flock of canaries. I was surprised at the tip she was drawing. They must have thought someone was dying.

When she finished, I didn't have to start the applause. It started itself. I picked up the coffee can, and paper money floated down like a shower of leaves.

When the tip cleared, three guys in greasy red sweatbands around their heads stood glaring at me. They looked about fourteen, and they looked like trouble. One of them slowly came forward until we were practically nose to nose.

"That's my coffee can," he kind of growled.

I had long basketball legs and figured I could outrun them. So I ducked and took off, and Holly gave a scream right out of some German opera. I ran smack into Bumpy Rhoades, who had sauntered over. I didn't know whether he had an ear for music or had heard Holly's cry for help.

Those constrictor muscles under his shirt swelled up. He juggled the sappy muggers straight into the sand, heads first. It didn't take them long to figure out they had done something stupid. They scuttled off like migrating crabs.

"Thanks," I said.

"Thank you," Holly added, in a small echo.

"You got yourself a fast-footed hat man," he said to her.

"Holly, his name's Bumpy," I said, by way of formal introduction. "Bumpy Rhoades."

"And you've got some voice, Miss Soprano," he remarked, smiling. "That's the only time I heard the 'Bell Song' without the bells."

He seemed to know Holly's kind of music, and that surprised me. Her, too. She gave him, practically a stranger, a smile.

"Her name's Holly Gomez," I said.

"Chickadee Gomez," my sister declared, correcting me.

My eyebrows must have shot up like window shades. Chickadee? Where had a crazy name like that come from? Those show-off birds back home? My sister had gone nuts. And then my eyebrows came back down. Didn't I say that Holly was brilliant? The Toad would never catch on to a show-off name like that. And it would look great in lights. CHICKADEE GOMEZ, world-famous opera star.

"How about dinner tonight?" Bumpy asked.

"Sure," I said.

"I meant your sister."

"Sure," Chickadee said.

And that's how Bumpy became our friend.

He began loaning me his library card. It turned out that Bumpy Rhoades was just a boardwalk name. He was really Mackenzie Birch, and no wonder he could juggle Latin as well as watermelons. He was a medical student at UCLA. The flying watermelons, he said, were putting him through college. And when he ran out of money, he could eat the act.

Every few nights or so he'd invite us and everybody else at Casa de Sueños to join him on the beach. We stood around eating his watermelons before they went bad and he had to replace them. It was summer dripping down my chin.

One night I found myself looking at Holly and wondering how our tears had dried so fast after our mother disappeared. It had only been four months. Was that enough? Shouldn't I feel guilty when I wasn't crying?

We had done plenty of that. I supposed we could thank the Toad for changing the subject on us. He was scaring us too much to hang on to all that darkness at home. Once we'd hit the road and left the city limits, we could take deep breaths. Once we'd crossed the state line, we could even begin to feel larkish. Now Holly was singing again.

It got to be July, and our boardwalk act took on a little class. Holly—that is, I mean, Chickadee—started putting on lipstick again. She bought a black opera hat, and I threw away the coffee can. The tips got better at once. It's as if the classy hat announced a rise in prices. And people kept coming back to stand around and listen to Chickadee. Even some on Rollerblades.

They'd ask her if she could sing Puccini or Verdi, and she would. It baffled me that there were crowds of people who knew all that noisy stuff.

Someone stole Chickadee's rusty VW off the street. We had left a few things in the car, including my soccer ball and some kids' books I hadn't wanted to leave behind in Albuquerque. Holly refused to report it to the police. She'd have to leave our real name, and we weren't dropping any markers for the Toad to find.

"Furthermore," she said, "we don't need to go anywhere. We are right where we want to be, aren't we? That beach is flypaper, with people like us stuck to it. You got something against blue sky and seagulls, Pep?"

MAN IN A WHITE SUIT

5

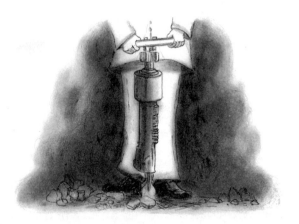

We did a lot of jogging along the surf in the mornings when the boardwalk traffic was light. Holly liked to run, trailing a green scarf from her neck. She kept checking her breathing against the stopwatch, and I kept an eye out for basketball and soccer games.

From time to time I hung around the beach parking lots if I saw some guys with a ball. Nobody invited me in at first, so I just watched.

But when I let it be known that my name was Gomez, they figured I was born with a soccer ball under my arm and waved me in. I was good and getting better. I had learned from watching Holly that you had to work at things or you'd just be average.

We had plenty of time to explore around, especially the canals behind the beach area. Some real-estate man had had them dug about a hundred years ago so he could sell house lots on the water. Now the canals looked like flooded streets with narrow cracked sidewalks. Small wooden houses were crowded along the banks. But there were some grand homes, too, and we'd heard some movie stars lived there.

We were window shopping on the mall in Santa Monica up the coast about a mile when Holly got homesick. At an out-of-town newspaper stand she had spotted a copy of the *Albuquerque Journal* and bought it. And wouldn't you know it, she read something we didn't really want to know about.

"Look at this," Holly said, and I figured someone had died. But that wasn't it at all.

A creep had slipped into our old house on the Heights and torn up the walls. He'd even jackhammered the cement slab garage floor.

Even though we had walked away from it, it made me mad that someone had trashed our home. I wondered what my old room looked like now. The police said that the burglar was obviously in search of something. But what? We hadn't left anything behind worth digging for.

"The Toad," Holly said sharply, and I watched her face go white, the way an octopus changes color when it is frightened.

Our neighbors had got suspicious about a man in a rumpled white suit hanging around and then, hearing all the jackhammer noise, they called the cops.

"At least we know what the Toad looks like now," I said.

"Man in a white suit? That doesn't tell us much," Holly replied.

"What do you suppose he was looking for? Tearing up our floor and all?"

"China, maybe. Termites."

"But why our place?" I asked.

We left the questions hanging in the air. There didn't seem to be any answer. Hanging in the air, just like that other question about our mother. Was she alive somehow? Mom was kind of famous for an archaeologist. They don't usually get their names in the papers, but she did. She was on a dig in Mexico when an earthquake struck. Her body has never been found.

We flew down there, Holly and me, and spent a lot

of time looking and asking around. Finally there was nothing to do but pack up her clothes and stuff and try to stop crying.

We kept muttering about the possibility that Mom would turn up. Maybe she hadn't been caught in the earthquake, in a cave that collapsed on top of her. I even began to think that maybe bandits kidnapped her for ransom.

Holly had shaken her head. "Where's the ransom note?"

"Maybe the bandits don't know how to write." You couldn't expect bandits to skip a couple of grades, the way I had.

As the months passed, Holly seemed to know that Mom was never coming back. I did, too. Kind of. Holly said our mother would want us to get on with our lives, and I knew that was true. But we didn't know how to do that until the Toad came along.

GETTING FAMOUS

6

HAVE YOU SEEN THEM?

The tap dancer moved out of Casa de Sueños, and we never did see who it was. "It's always hello and good-bye around here," Miss Fiesta said.

A girl about my age, named Daisy, moved in with her mother, who turned out to be the Statue of Liberty woman. Daisy had braces on her teeth and seemed embarrassed about it. She kept pretty much to herself, so I wasn't really getting to know her. She drew in a book a lot but wouldn't let me see anything.

Holly and I were eating dinner on our laps and watching television when I said, "Holly, I bet I figured out why the Toad was stalking us."

She gave me a tired look. "Pep, we've got to get him out of our heads. It's what he wants, to keep dogging us, wherever we are."

"Maybe he just wanted to scare us into clearing out. Then he could jackhammer through the floor to find whatever he was looking for."

"There's nothing under all that cement but rocks and dirt and red ants," Holly said.

"But maybe he doesn't know that."

After a couple of days, it was easy to stop thinking about him. The sun rose every morning like a happy face. You could hear the waves breaking on the beach and giving off little clapping sounds. Sounds like applause, I said to Holly.

"Applause for what?"

"For our presto-chango act. We turned ourselves from desert rats into beach bums, didn't we?"

I should have known better than to start feeling cocky about outwitting the Toad.

A couple of days later Daisy came up to me in the hall and showed me my picture on a piece of junk mail.

"Is that you?"

I froze. It was my picture and Holly's picture side by side under a question:

HAVE YOU SEEN THEM?

It was a missing-children flyer with our ages and heights and hair colors. It said that we were missing from Albuquerque, New Mexico. I snatched it out of her hand.

"No, it's not me. Us, I mean. We're not missing."

I rolled up the flyer and tossed it in the kitchen trash. T. Tex Rimbo was typing away in the patio, and I wondered if he had seen it. When Daisy had gone, I dug the thing out and showed it to Holly.

She was drinking coffee out of a paper cup and just about spilled it. "The Toad!" she exclaimed.

"Yeah."

We stood there for a long time, frozen. Finally, I said, "If all he wanted was to trash our house, why does he care where we flew off to?"

"He's still stalking us," Holly muttered. "You said Daisy recognized us?"

"Kind of. They're old pictures. I denied everything."

"The Toad must have found them in our attic," Holly said.

And I said, "Do we run?"

Steam was practically coming out of her ears. "I'm tired of running," Holly declared. "Follow me."

HIDING IN PLAIN SIGHT

7

We rushed out, and Holly bought some stuff to bleach our hair. When our heads dried, we were blond as haystacks. Holly looked pretty razzle-dazzle. You might think her name really was Chickadee. I looked as if I had slept with my head in a jar of mustard. She even did my eyebrows.

We stayed clear of the boardwalk and the other performers who had gotten to know us. At first we hardly left Casa de Sueños. How do you turn yourself invisible? We had money enough to eat and pay the rent for a while, but not enough to buy another car and keep moving.

In a couple of weeks, Holly figured, everyone would

forget the faces on the flyer. When we had to go outside, we smeared our noses with white gunk to keep from getting burned and draped towels over our heads the way you do when your hair is wet. That way we could hide in plain sight.

T. Tex Rimbo was up to his baseball cap in potato bugs and didn't seem to even notice that we had gone platinum.

I avoided Daisy. I did go to the library a lot because nobody looked at anybody there, just books. I ran into Daisy reading at a table. She amazed me by giving me a smile, revealing the weldings on her teeth, and talking as if we were old friends.

"What happened to your hair?" she asked.

"Search me," I answered. "I woke up the other morning, looked in the mirror, and there it was."

"I look like I'm chewing on a birdcage, don't I?"

"What are you talking about?"

"The braces on my teeth."

"They look okay," I said.

"They look dreadful. What are you reading?"

"*The Wolves of Willoughby Chase.*"

"I read it three times. Have you read Tolkien's *Lord of the Rings?*"

"I'm trying to read every other book in the library," I said. "I skip around but haven't tackled the Ts yet."

"You like poetry?"

"Only when I can understand it," I said. "I like Poe. 'The Raven' and things like that."

"Poe is weird. He scares me."

"I gotta go."

She spread open the book she was looking it. "It's poems for two voices. You need someone to read along with you. Want to try it?"

"Sure. But not right now."

And I left, kind of flustered. Why was she being so friendly all of a sudden? She might be thinking about turning in Holly and me. She looked suspicious to me. I wasn't going to let her trip me up.

At the beach nobody gave Holly and me a second look. By late afternoon the sun worshipers cleared out, and Holly would open her mouth. She'd sing for the seagulls. They must have been deaf. With some notes the area under her chin would vibrate as if she had a live hummingbird under her tongue.

Most of the time I dug my feet in the sand and read a library book. I discovered that no matter how hot the sand was, if you dug your feet below the surface, it was cooler.

If you dug even deeper, it got absolutely cold. I didn't need a book to tell me the white sand reflected the heat. I thought about the cave that had collapsed in the earthquake. It must have felt cool, too. To Mom.

I had a book from the library, a book on archaeology with colored pictures that Mom had had at home. I figured that was I what might do when I grew up: get a pick and dig up ancient cities. But maybe not. There were baseball and soccer. Or if I grew tall enough, I might go into basketball. I hadn't entirely forgiven archaeology for taking Mom away.

Sometimes I read around in the notebook she was keeping on her last dig in Mexico. I didn't care so much about her field notes, but I liked running my eyes over her tiny handwriting in the green ink she liked. It felt like a small hug.

She had gone down there on the trail of the famous Seven Lost Cities of Cíbola. There was a crazy rumor that those cities were practically solid gold.

I grew up hearing that stuff. Before John Wayne began shooting things up out west, a bunch of dusty Spanish explorers came galloping up from Mexico—conquistadors, they were called. Conquerors. They were led by a rich guy named Don Francisco Coronado. He rode around in golden armor. "Flashing like a bonfire on horseback," my mother told me with a laugh. He must have knocked everybody's eyes out.

Those conquerors were so greedy they couldn't see straight. They heard rumors of seven Indian cities so crusted over with gold and silver and jewels that they'd need skip loaders to cart the stuff away.

So here came the conquistadors in their hot armor, rattling like tin cans across the desert. All they ever found were some muddy Zuñi pueblos, not worth two cents.

But my mother did uncover a suit of Coronado's gold armor, and that made the news. It got stolen, and that made the news, too. I didn't believe in curses, but if I did, I'd think that armor had a curse on it. It had lured Mom to Mexico, hadn't it?

In a week or so Chickadee was singing on the boardwalk again. We kind of forgot about the Toad. And then the phone rang in the downstairs hall, and our landlady gave a shout up.

"Miss Chickadee, it's for you!"

Holly looked at me. And I looked at her.

We didn't know anybody except Bumpy Rhoades,

and he was in the patio with his nose in a medical book. Who was calling?

"The Toad?" Holly muttered, turning white.

"Yeah," I said, nodding sharply.

The Toad had found us. Must be. Someone had turned us in.

"Say we moved out," Holly shouted down the stairs. "Hang up."

The phone rang again around ten the next morning, and that's when we began to pack our stuff. Miss Fiesta climbed up the stairs and barged in.

"What's with you? You got a thing about talking on the phone? I've got a thing about climbing the stairs to tell you the phone's for you."

"Just hang up," Holly said.

"Someone's awful anxious to meet you."

"I'll bet."

"You packing?"

I said, "That man on the phone's bothering us."

Miss Fiesta looked at us with one eye crimped and the other peering down the side of her nose. "There's no man on the phone. Sounds like a lady to me."

"A lady?" Holly said. "You sure?"

"That voice is wearing high heels, Chickadee, dear.

Shall I tell her you left town without paying the rent?"

"I'll take it. And our rent is paid up."

Holly went to the phone, and I saw her face go all aglow as if she had swallowed a sunrise. She sputtered, and her eyelashes beat like butterflies, and she kept saying, "Yes . . . yes . . . yes . . . of course . . . yes . . . yes!"

When she hung up and turned to me, I said, "Bad news, huh?"

"Now what's this about a guy bothering you?" asked Miss Fiesta.

"Never mind him!" Holly exclaimed. "They want me to sing *La Bohème!*"

"Who does?" I asked.

"Some people are forming the Venice-on-the-Beach Opera Company. That was the director, Liz Anne Wilber-Jones."

"Oh, I know her," Miss Fiesta put in. "She's that golden-haired ex-countess who lives over on the canals. Real gold, I wouldn't be surprised."

Holly was practically breaking into song. "Someone heard me on the boardwalk, and she's been trying to track me down. They're going to put up a tent on the beach and do opera. Would I care to audition for the part of Musetta?"

"Is that the lead?" Miss Fiesta asked.

"No," Holly answered. "But close enough."

Miss Fiesta pursed her lips. She must have figured Holly was too innocent for the situation and needed a mother hen. "I'll go to the audition with you. You'll get the lead."

THE HOUSE ON THE CANAL

8

The house on the canal seemed right out of the Grimms' fairy tales. It had turrets that looked like red onions and rounded windows and a porch all hung with wooden lace.

We walked in on blazing Oriental carpets, Holly and Miss Fiesta and me. Ex-Countess Liz Anne Wilber-Jones was waiting for us at the grand piano. That piano seemed as long as a bus.

"They tell me you have a lovely voice," she said.

Miss Fiesta, looking like a sumo wrestler in a feathered hat, burst right in. "Voice? She could teach canaries."

"I'll be the judge of that," answered the ex-countess.

She wore earrings that swung around like wrecking balls when she turned her head. Her hair did look like spun gold. "Miss Gomez, is it? We were well into rehearsals when one of our sopranos abandoned us. Moved to Juneau, Alaska, the silly girl. So we find ourselves short one soprano, Miss Gomez. Let's hear you do a bit of Puccini. Do you know Musetta's waltz, the showstopper in the second act?"

Holly nodded. "I know it. English or Italian?"

"*Quando me'n vo'soletta per la via,*" answered the opera director with a swing of her earrings. She began to play. Holly sang in Italian.

She looked so nervous, I could hardly watch her. But she kept her mouth open and sang right through to the end. It sounded okay to me, even if I didn't understand a word of it.

The woman said nothing, trying Holly on another song and another. By that time Holly's hands had stopped trembling, but she looked worried. Still, whatever song the countess turned to, Holly knew the words, some in French. I saw her tongue vibrating a lot, and I figured that was a good sign.

Suddenly the lady stopped playing, jumped up, and began poking Holly in the back and stomach as if she suspected appendicitis. "You're developing muscles. Good. Who is your teacher, Miss Gomez?"

"I don't have one just now."

"Why not?"

"I can't afford one."

"That's no excuse. You have a heavenly pianissimo. By some miracle you have not ruined it by dabbling around on your own. But you must learn to allow the song to float on your breath. I will teach you. Be back tomorrow afternoon at two, and we will start."

I watched Holly's eyes widen. I guess mine did, too.

Miss Fiesta felt it was time to speak up. "We came about that part in the opera show you're putting on? You passing on her, countess?"

The woman closed the piano. "She will play the part of Mimì."

Our landlady didn't let Holly get a word in. "We're not singing any supporting roles. You said yourself she has a superb pianissimo, whatever that is."

"That's true."

"Well?" By that time Holly was practically shoving Miss Fiesta and me out of the room.

"As Miss Gomez knows," said the ex-countess, "Mimì is the starring role."

THE CRYSTAL BALL

9

Holly seemed in shock for the rest of the day. She told the amazing news to Bumpy Rhoades, who was sitting in the patio studying a medical book on the spinal column. They got all excited and decided to have dinner on the beach to celebrate. That's when I noticed Daisy hanging around, looking lonely.

I tried not to notice her. Had she really believed my story that we weren't the faces on the missing-persons thing? And then I thought, what was wrong with me? If we became friends, she might think again about turning us in.

"It's a picnic," I said. "You wanna come?"

"Sure."

We spread towels near the surf and ate pizzas. Everyone watched the sun go down, ooing and ahhing as if it had never done that before. The tide was coming in, and the waves were bouncing along and making an awful racket.

After a while Daisy said, "You want me to read your fortune?"

"I guess so," I said.

I figured she was going to pull a greasy deck of cards out of her beach bag, but she didn't. She pulled out a glass ball about the size of a cantaloupe.

"It's a crystal ball. My mother used it to tell fortunes at parties."

"Does the thing work?"

Daisy came as close to smiling as she cared to with all that iron in her mouth. "My mom never could see anything in it. It got kind of spooky, so she quit and became the Statue of Liberty."

"Well, have a look, just in case," I said.

"What do you want to know?"

"Can you see a guy in a white suit in there?"

"I'll check."

She gazed into the crystal for a long time. Then she said, "Let's try something else."

"Let me have a look."

I gazed into the ball for all I was worth, but all I could see was nothing. "It must be broken."

Now Daisy really let out a laugh. "Don't you know fortune-telling is make-believe, Gomez? My mother told me she used to make up all that stuff she told people. She dreamed up nice things, of course, and that made people feel good. Trouble was, people believed her, so she cut up her gypsy dress and made me a skirt and two blouses."

I kept staring into the crystal ball as if the man in the white suit were lurking in there to prove Daisy wrong. But he was keeping way out of sight. "You can call me Pep," I said.

"If you're not from Albuquerque, where are you from?"

An alarm began to buzz in my head. If she remembered Albuquerque, she must still be thinking about us.

"We're from all over," I answered. "We keep traveling."

"Like Mom and me. But I was born in Berkeley. You know where that is, don't you? Across the bay from San Francisco?"

"Of course," I said, even though I was a little vague about the geography.

She had been drawing with a stick in the sand, and I saw a figure of a man. "Who's that supposed to be?" I asked.

"A man in a white suit," she answered.

THE SPEAR-CARRIER
10

Holly went to her singing lessons every afternoon and kind of lost interest in the boardwalk. But we had to eat, so on weekends we set up our act across from the Statue of Liberty. Sometimes Daisy hung around her mother, but she was too shy to work the crowds with a tin can in her hand. I'd usually see her with her feet in the sand, reading a book.

Holly brought home lots of news about the ex-countess. "She used to be a big opera star until she retired. She got twenty-seven curtain calls at the Licio in Barcelona. She did *Carmen* at La Scala in Milan. She sang with Pavarotti!"

"Is that good?" I asked.

She gave me a scornful look and began shaving her legs. "Not exactly a steam whistle, Pavarotti. Only the voice of the century."

"Better than the Sawtooth Mountain Boys?"

She rolled her eyes. "You're hopeless, Kevin."

"Pep," I said, correcting her.

And then rehearsals resumed for the Venice-on-the-Beach Opera Company. Only it wasn't on the beach yet. Rehearsals were held in an abandoned gym on Main Street.

I hung around a lot when I wasn't at the library or playing soccer. I watched the tenor, who was going to sing the part of a starving playwright. Holly was supposed to fall in love with him, when she wasn't coughing. Boy, was she sick. The story dealt with a lot of artist types who live in an attic in Paris in the dead of winter. I figured it was something like Casa de Sueños, but without the sunshine and avocados.

I was getting burned up at the tenor, whose name was Jonah and who worked in a car wash. He seemed to be trying to push himself forward all the time as if Holly—Chickadee to the opera world—were in his way.

The wrecking balls hanging from ex-Countess Liz

Anne Wilber-Jones's ears kept swinging around as she played the piano and directed the singers. She didn't say anything to Jonah, but I figured before long she was going to turn into a whale and swallow Jonah alive.

"We need a couple of spear-carriers in the second act," she announced.

Holly lifted an arm and pointed straight at me.

"My brother, Pep," she said.

Me? Where did she get that air-headed idea? Once I tried to sing "Row, Row, Row Your Boat," and the boat sank. But the next thing I knew, the ex-countess had my arm and was dragging me along an imaginary street with imaginary sidewalk tables on it.

"A toy seller will enter, and you and a few other kids just frolic along. You've got a friend or two to fill in, haven't you?"

It turned out a spear-carrier was just an extra, like Miss Fiesta was in the movies. You didn't actually carry a spear. You were just a live body. The last thing ex-Countess Liz Anne Wilber-Jones wanted me to do was sing.

I couldn't find Daisy the next day to make her a spear-carrier, too. She wasn't in the library, but as long as I was there, I'd pick up a book I was after. I couldn't find it and was about to go up to the librarian when one of the guys who had jumped me on the boardwalk came over to me. Suddenly he was in my face.

"Your name Gomez?" he asked.

"Yes," I said.

"So is mine," he said. "Don't tell anybody you saw me in here. Understand?"

"Ruin your reputation, huh?"

"Dummy up. Get me?"

"Got you."

And he left. I felt a little as if I'd been sideswiped by a speeding car. He sure didn't want his friends to know he could read.

The librarian was a substitute, for I'd never seen him before. He must have overheard Gomez talking to me. When I said I couldn't find a copy of *Frankenstein* on the shelf, he kind of dismissed me with a quick glance. "Did you look under R. L. Stine, Gomez?"

"No," I said. "I was looking under Shelley, Mary Wollstonecraft. She wrote it, didn't she?"

Did he think because my name was Gomez, I couldn't read above the third-grade level? I felt insulted for the real Gomez, who had just sideswiped me. For all I knew, he was reading Shakespeare, though I figured that was a stretch.

It turned out they didn't have a copy of *Frankenstein* at that branch but would get one if I'd leave my name. I didn't want to do that, so I left.

On the boardwalk I sidled up to the Statue of Liberty. "Mrs. Niederhauser," I said, "can you tell me where Daisy is?"

The Statue of Liberty didn't answer. There were people walking by and tossing coins and bills into the draperies at her feet. I guess she considered it undignified for the Statue of Liberty to have a hat man.

I must have had to wait for five minutes before there was a break in the crowd. She didn't move her lips at all, but she parted them. Then she spoke like a ventriloquist.

"At the dentist. There's a fly buzzing around my nose, Pep. If you don't shoo it off, you're going to see the Statue of Liberty sneeze."

I banished the fly and wandered back to Casa de Sueños. I sat in the shade of the patio, under the avocado tree, and waited for Daisy to come home.

STANDING STILL

11

hile I was waiting, I got a brainstorm. With her lessons and the rehearsal and the opera score to learn, Holly had less and less time for the boardwalk. She said she didn't know how she was going to pay the rent.

I got to thinking about Daisy's mom and the Statue of Liberty. How much talent did it take to do a mannequin act? All you had to do was stand still and keep from blinking your eyes.

I figured I could make more than working for Bumpy and help Holly pay the rent. Maybe I'd be Frankenstein's monster. I'd wear big shoes nailed to blocks of two-byfours. Holly could make up my head with some bloody scars and a couple of fake bolts through my neck.

I struck a pose in the patio. I held out my arms in front of me and froze. I stopped blinking my eyes.

Bumpy Rhoades came walking in and said, "Hi, Pep."

I ignored him. Ants could have been climbing up my legs, and I wouldn't even have twitched. He grabbed my wrist and began taking my pulse.

"Hmmm," he murmured. "I suspect mad cow disease. Let me hear you moo."

I felt so ridiculous, it was hard not to burst out laughing. But I remained motionless until he went away. And then I blinked.

My arms felt heavy as pig iron. They were beginning to hurt. I had to drop them and work them around. This pose wasn't going to work. I started over.

I crossed my arms this time. That was a lot more comfortable, but my eyes kept wanting to blink. I tried staring into space, the way the Statue of Liberty did, but the eyes were going to take practice. I supposed I could get Holly's stopwatch and time myself between blinks.

Finally I had to shut my eyes and give them a rest.

That's when Daisy came up and seemed to catch on. "Who are you supposed to be?"

"Frankenstein walking in his sleep," I said. "How does your mother keep her eyes from blinking?"

"She kind of goes into a trance and concentrates on memorizing all of Shakespeare. She's into *Midsummer Night's Dream* right now."

A trance? How do you do that? I was beginning to lose my enthusiasm for a career as a mannequin and opened my eyes. That's when I saw that Daisy was smiling as if she were showing off a new car.

Only it was her teeth she wanted me to see.

"What happened to your braces?" I blurted out as if I didn't know.

"Gone to junk heaven."

"Your teeth sure are straight."

"Thanks," she said.

"They'll look great onstage."

"What are you talking about?"

"In my sister's opera. They need you and me to be spear-carriers in the second act."

"Not me," Daisy said firmly.

"We won't have to sing. Maybe hum a little."

"Not me. Not ever."

"But you can smile all you want."

She gave her head a tilt. "Okay," she said.

RETURN OF THE TARANTULAS

12

With all the stuff she had to do, Holly wasn't getting a lot of sleep. That opera job wouldn't pay a cent unless they sold a lot of tickets, but that didn't bother her. It would be a big experience to sing in a real opera. Maybe someone would see her.

"Someone from the cinema?" I asked. I was already beginning to talk like a Californian.

"Movies? You want to blast my career?" she answered, nose in the air, but grinning, too. She began to brush her teeth.

"Holly," I said suddenly, "how come you never want to talk about Mom anymore?"

She stopped and looked at me, toothbrush in midair. "I thought you didn't want to."

"I don't. But I do."

"Anything you want to say, I'm listening."

"What if she's not really dead?"

She rinsed out her mouth. "We've been over that a thousand times, Kevin."

"I know."

"We've got to get used to it. If Mom were alive, she'd have phoned us."

"But what if bandits were holding her for ransom?"

"Then they'd have phoned us."

I shook my head. "They wouldn't know how to reach us."

"Kevin, you keep talking bandits. If it makes you feel better to imagine bandits, imagine away. But I've got to holler quits for both of us."

"Why?" I asked.

"Because Mom wouldn't want us moping around all the time the way we did back home."

I said, "Holly?"

"Yes?"

"Mom could have amnesia. You can get that from a hit on the head."

"It's possible."

"But you don't believe it," I said.

"No."

"But if she did have amnesia and came to, how'd she find us?"

"She couldn't."

"That's what I thought."

Then Holly gave me a clownish smile, with toothpaste around her lips. "But if she does have amnesia, and came to in the hands of bandits, guess what?"

"What?"

"She'd also want you to brush your teeth."

We made some money on weekends, when Holly figured she couldn't pass up the big crowds on the boardwalk. But the rest of the week I hardly saw her unless I sat around the gym and watched *La Bohème* shaping up.

"More voice! Voice!" ex-Countess Liz Anne Wilber-Jones would call out to Holly, meaning she should sing a little louder. And the tenor, Jonah, would kind of smirk, as if Holly were being punished.

A moment later, though, the ex-countess banged the piano, lost her temper, and leaped to her feet. "Jonah, sir!

If the part called for a tenor leading a cavalry charge, I would have engaged a bugler! The poet-slash-playwright Rodolfo—that's the part you are playing, don't forget—is falling gently in love with Mimì. Do stop trying to shatter windows with your voice. We will not be passing out earmuffs at each performance. Now let's try the duet again, and find a balance. And if I hear anyone again call this opera La Boheem, you're dismissed. In the civilized world, it is pronounced La *Bo-ehm*. Everyone got that?"

When Daisy came along, she brought her sketchbook. That's how I discovered she had made a sketch of me. There I was, before Holly bleached my hair, looking like the missing-child picture.

"What did you do that for?" I asked uneasily.

"Do what?"

"Draw me. That was sneaky."

"What are you getting angry about?"

"Did you show that picture to anyone? Your mother?"

"None of your business," Daisy replied, getting red in the face. She tore the picture out of her book, ripped it up, and handed the pieces to me. "Here, you can have it."

"I don't want it," I said, handing them back.

She got up and dropped the pieces in the trash barrel and walked out. The picture had kind of rattled me, reminding me that Holly and I were hiding in plain sight. But did I really think we had something to fear from Daisy? If she were going turn us in, she'd have done it when she first saw the missing-children flyer. I ought to apologize about the picture.

I got up to follow her, but outside I ran into trouble. There stood the other Gomez with two of his friends, one of them with freckles and yellow hair that stuck up in spikes. All of them wore red headbands, as if their scalps were bleeding.

"Hey, Gomez," called out Gomez. "Maybe we're cousins."

"I don't think so," I said.

"We're the Tarantulas Gang. Ever hear of us?"

"I have now."

"We'll let you in," he said with a fixed smirk. "We'll let you join. Right, Spike? Right, Tony? You wanna run with us? Or you wanna get your legs broke?"

I tried to look honored to meet such big-time weirdos and said, "Gee, I'd like to, Gomez, but I don't want to make trouble for you."

"Trouble? We make the trouble."

I shook my head with mock disappointment. "Naw, it's my friend on the beach—you remember, the big gringo with the short temper? The last gang I joined, he put everybody in the hospital. That was six months ago, and two of them are still there."

The Tarantulas looked at one another, shrugged, spit, and then ambled off.

Daisy was gone. Run off. I ended up at the Statue of Liberty and said, "Tell Daisy I really liked the picture she drew. It looked just like me."

Not a word out of the Statue. I gazed across the way at a fortune-teller reading someone's palm. I could do that, couldn't I? It was all made-up stuff, wasn't it? Just beach entertainment, like face painting and merry-go-rounds?

"Mrs. Niederhauser, could I borrow your crystal ball? I won't do any harm. I'll just make up good fortunes. I've got to make some money."

That night there was a soft knock at the door. It was Daisy carrying the crystal ball.

"I really liked the picture you drew," I said.

"It wasn't so good."

"Good? You gone blind, Daisy? It looked so much like me, I thought it was a mirror. That's what scared me."

"What do you want the crystal ball for?" she asked.

"Daisy, you're so good at art. Would you make up a big sign that says PEPE, THE WORLD'S YOUNGEST FORTUNE-TELLER?"

She looked at me, and for a moment her blue eyes opened wider. "You think anyone's going to believe a kid?"

"I could be a prodigy, like Mozart. Wasn't he giving piano concerts when he was still in diapers?"

"Not quite."

I said, "Put the word FREE in big letters on the sign."

"How you going to make any money if it's free?"

"You can pass the hat, Daisy."

"Not me."

"Then you can shill. Pretend to be a customer. Will you paint the sign?"

"Okay." Then she turned at the door and faced me again. "Your name's not really Pepe, is it?"

THE TAROT CARDS

13

I borrowed Bumpy Rhoades's library card again and checked the shelves to see if there was anything on how to be a fortune-teller. All I could find was a book on palmistry.

It was full of diagrams of the human hand with the lines given names. The big chief seemed to be the one running from the wrist toward the first finger, called the lifeline. That was supposed to tell you how long you would live. Really? Wouldn't you have to be nuts to believe that? How was a line in your hand supposed to know about an earthquake in Mexico and cut itself short?

But that night, while Holly was wrapping her wet hair in a towel, I looked up from the book. "I wish we had a picture of Mom's hand."

"What are you talking about?"

"It says here you can tell how long a person will live by looking at the creases in her hand. If Mom has a long lifeline, she'll have a long life. She'll still be alive."

"Kevin—"

"If the line's short, it means—"

Holly gave me a weary, sad look. "Okay if we change the subject?"

"We brought some pictures," I persisted. "Maybe there's something showing her hand."

"Of course not." Holly peered at me as if my brains were going soft. "What are you reading?"

"Never mind. I mean skip it. Forget it."

I returned the library book. I figured you had to believe the world was flat to buy that moldy old stuff. There were even secrets of figuring out the future by looking at the lines in your foot. How do you spell weird?

But fortune-tellers all along the boardwalk were as common as hamburger joints. Most of them sat shuffling tarot cards under signs hung about, proclaiming they knew all and told all.

So I stopped in front of an old lady named Princess Zulisa. She was wearing a lot of black lace. She had tired eyes and a dried-up face like the inside of a walnut. If anyone could see into the future and teach me what to say, it had to be Princess Zulisa.

"How much?" I asked.

"Whatever you care to donate, child."

Child? We were getting off to a bum start. But I sat down at her card table and she handed me her deck of cards. They were covered with brightly colored pictures of old-time knights and moons and queens and jesters and stars and whatnots.

"Shuffle the cards seven times," she said in a tired, crabby voice. I don't think she was thrilled to have a kid for a customer. How much of a donation did she calculate I could leave? She viewed me, I thought, as a charity case. She explained, "That will shuffle your spirit into the tarot cards, sonny."

Sonny. Did she think I was wearing short pants? I'd remember not to make my customers feel small.

The cards were larger than regular playing cards and hard to shuffle. While I was at it, she began asking me questions.

"You worried about school?" she mumbled.

"No."

"You lost something? A pocket knife?"

"No," I said.

"You want your folks to stop yelling at you?"

"No."

For a woman who was supposed to understand all and tell you things, she didn't know much. I could make bum guesses, too. Then, to my surprise, I heard myself blurt out, "What about the man in the white suit?"

I felt the hair on my neck stiffen. Was I falling for this hokey-pokey stuff? Then I gave a small shrug. Worth a try, wasn't it?

"Man in a white suit," she repeated. "A relative?"

"No."

"A friend?"

"No."

"What's his name?"

"I don't know. Can the cards tell me?"

She didn't answer. She took the cards out of my hands, gave them three cuts, and turned a card faceup. It showed a picture of a jester.

"The Fool," she explained.

"What does that mean?" I asked.

"We shall see."

She turned over another card. This one showed a man hanging upside down from a tree.

"The Hanging Man," she said. "That's good."

Good? I wondered.

She dealt several cards in a semicircle on the table and studied them. Then she pounced with a bent finger on a card showing the sun with all its golden rays. "Splendid, sonny. Luck. You are in luck. Luck awaits you."

I made a mental note. Luck. Spread it on like margarine.

"The Fool is a traveler. You will travel. You will meet new friends to hang on your tree of life. But I can hear the Fool whispering the letter C to me. You know someone whose name begins with a C?"

I couldn't think of anyone. But then the name Coronado sprung up in my mind. "I guess so," I said.

"Of course. The cards never lie. You will receive a letter. Perhaps it will be from C."

Not likely. Coronado had been dead for over four hundred years.

"What about the man in the white suit?" I asked.

She tapped a finger on the Hanging Man. "Your friend is upside down, too."

What did that mean? That the Toad was in Australia?

"But what's his name?" I asked.

"I will work on it."

I wondered if she was trying to rope me into coming back for another reading. Out of the corner of my eye I saw Bumpy Rhoades watching me with a big laugh on his face.

Princess Zulisa scooped up the cards to announce that the session was over. I left a dollar bill, and she gave a little screech. "I usually get fifteen dollars for a reading, sonny! Can't you make it five?"

"Can't," I said, and walked away.

Bumpy Rhoades was waiting for me with his fists on his hips.

"I didn't figure you for a mark," he said.

"What's that?"

"A sucker. Don't you know telling the future is bunk?"

"Of course I do," I said defensively. "But she did get one thing right. She said I knew someone whose name started with a C, and I do."

"You and everybody else."

"I'm just trying to learn the ropes," I said.

"You going to be a beach Nostradamus, like the rest of these jokers?"

"Just for fun," I explained.

"Your sister will kill you—just for fun."

Maybe I better not let her see me, I thought.

"I'm still looking for a hat man," he said.

I gave a little shrug and said nothing. If fortune-telling turned out to be a bust, I was glad to know I had a career with the hat. I didn't need a crystal ball to tell me I wasn't going to have much of a future unless I got some talent. But I couldn't juggle like Bumpy or sing like Holly or draw like Daisy. What was out there waiting for me? If I knew a good fortune-teller, I'd ask.

I BECOME A
FORTUNE-TELLER

14

Pepe,
the World's Youngest
Fortune Teller

While Holly was having her lesson with ex-Countess Liz Anne, I borrowed a card table and a couple of folding chairs from Casa de Sueños. Carrying the crystal ball, Daisy followed me until I found a shady spot to tell my first fortune.

"Who was Nostradamus?" I asked.

"Don't you know?"

"Of course. But I forgot."

"He's a Frenchman who made a lot of murky predictions hundreds of years ago."

I gave a little shrug. "Oh, *that* Nostradamus," I said.

"My mother has one of his books. She said he made

so many guesses, some were bound to come true. You like the sign?"

Daisy had used a lot of Chinese red paint to announce the world's youngest fortune-teller.

"Dazzling," I said, and hung it from a palm tree.

Then we waited around for customers to line up and have their fortunes told.

I had rehearsed what I would say. Like Princess Zulisa, I'd predict that a letter would be coming in the mail—that was a safe bet. And that there'd be a journey—everyone wanted to go on a trip, right? I figured the whole thing would be like doing card tricks. Just showbiz.

An hour went by. People gave us the eye as they passed and mostly smiled. If they were all looking to get famous in the movies, the way Bumpy Rhoades said, you'd think they'd want an advance peek at their casting chances. If wannabes asked me if they would end up on the cutting-room floor, I'd stall. I'd say I'd have to study the entrails of chickens, the way the old prophets did— and that I was plumb out of chickens.

I turned to Daisy, who was reading. She had decided to read every other library book that I was skipping. She had a novel by Leon Garfield, *Smith*, open on her lap.

"You ought to read this," she said. "It's about a kid something like you."

"He tells fortunes?"

"Not that bad. He only picks pockets."

"Funny," I said. "Anybody doesn't like my looks into the future, I'll hand 'em their money back. Sit in the chair and look like a customer."

As she sat down to shill, a wild-eyed woman came rushing along and yelled out, "Hey, one of my kids is lost! Look in that crazy ball and see where he is? Kid with a sunburned nose!"

I just about backed out of the fortune-telling business on the spot. But I had a second thought and gazed into the crystal ball. "I see the police station down the boardwalk. Go there and you'll find him."

She gave a quick sigh of relief. Didn't she know that the police station was the first place to look? "What do I owe you?" she asked.

"Nothing. Pepe, the world's youngest fortune-teller, is always glad to help."

And off she flew. When I looked up again, there stood Gomez, without his sidekicks, for once. He was wearing dark sunglasses that looked mad at the world.

"You tell fortunes?" he asked.

"Just for fun."

"Just for fun, you read my hand."

I shook my head. "I use a crystal ball."

"Does it work?"

"Probably not."

He flopped down. "What does it say about me? I'll be rich, eh? Live in a big house? Lots of servants?"

I looked into the ball to stall for time. Why not just tell him he'd have lots of luck and get a letter and go on a journey? Instead, I murmured, "You won't like what I see."

He pulled off his sunglasses. "Whaddya see?"

"Bars."

"Bicycle bars? Chocolate bars?"

"Jail bars," I said.

"Yeah? You see bars, you better see a hacksaw." He bent forward and his eyes almost smiled. "You foolin' with schoolin'? That thing don't compute."

"See for yourself."

He leaned closer, his nose almost touching the crystal ball. He took his time. Then he shook his head. "I don't see any jailhouse. I don't see any bars. You pulling my chain, amigo?"

I checked the ball and shook my head. "The picture

is gone," I said, kind of astonished. "Faded away. It was there a minute go. Clear as paint."

He didn't know whether to believe me or to start shoving me. Finally he picked up my empty top hat and fished his fingers around inside to check for money. He pulled the sunglasses back onto his nose.

"I'll come back," he said, as if it were a friendly threat. "Jail bars, eh?" He gave a shrug and ambled off.

Without realizing it, he had shilled for me, because another kid, eating cotton candy, sat right down. I told her she'd have lots of luck and that she'd get a letter in the mail and go on a trip. That made her happy, but not happy enough to throw any coins in my hat.

"The sign says free," she said.

By the time we folded our props, we had made only seven dollars and change. Considering how much happiness I had spread around, it was hardly worth the bother. I split the money with Daisy, since the crystal ball was hers. We dragged everything back home and rushed off to rehearsal on Main Street.

"Lovely news, everyone!" ex-Countess Liz Anne announced. "Opening night has been advanced. We sing in two weeks! Not much time to knock off the rough edges, is it? Between now and then, nobody sleeps! Costume fittings today—this is our costume designer, Miranda. Stand still and be measured."

So Holly got measured, and so did Daisy and I. I couldn't believe it—I was going to have to wear short pants. I was to play a kid following a toy seller across the stage. If it weren't for Holly, I would have junked show business on the spot. I was too tall for short pants. I was going to look like a Popsicle.

Holly began to cough a lot, and a couple of nights later I asked, "You sick, Holly?"

"Do I look sick?"

"You're coughing."

"I'm not coughing," she answered, hacking away. "I'm acting. In the opera Mimì is sick, remember, and she enters coughing. When she's not singing, she's coughing. The countess says I need more practice. Cough. Cough."

Some opera, I thought.

Early the next morning, as we were jogging along the beach, Holly said, "Listen to the ocean. Have you noticed all the opera sounds it makes?"

"Verdi and Puccini didn't write everything," I said as if the ocean needed someone to stick up for it.

"It's hissing. Like Iago in *Othello*. Sometimes it's the

booming cannons in the '1812 Overture.' You should notice things like that if you're going to be a writer."

"Me?" I stopped in my tracks. "Who says I'm going to be a writer?"

The surf washed in around our feet. "Mom did."

"Mom?"

"She told me your letters showed a kind of bouncy gift with words. She said you'd probably be a writer."

"How come I'm always the last to know?"

"Let's go."

A writer? I'd have to think about that. I figured I might be a lot of things. But an author? Wouldn't I have to learn to spell all the words in the dictionary? Of course, Mom could be wrong. I wasn't sure I wanted to be a writer.

I got another surprise when we were lifting free weights at Muscle Beach. Holly gave me a funny look and a giggle.

"Listen to you," she said.

"What?"

"You're humming grand opera. That was Rodolfo's aria from the first act."

"Horrors," I said.

GASP

15

R ehearsals ran through the weekend, so Holly couldn't work the boardwalk crowds. But I did, with my crystal ball act. I'd asked Daisy to change my name on the sign. She painted out Pepe and I became Nostradamus, Jr.

Business picked up, and I don't mean kids. Adults must have known about that old Frenchman because they sat right down. Even T. Tex Rimbo decided to have his fortune told.

"Can you see any potato bugs in that crystal, eh, Junior?"

I gave the ball my best gaze. "I see a letter coming—"

"Never mind the mail," he said, changing the direction of his baseball cap. "Is my screenplay going to strike it rich? See any dollar signs?"

"Nothing's coming through yet," I said.

He got up as suddenly as he had sat down. "Let me know when you hear from the future. I can't wait around."

He actually dropped a couple of dollars in my hat. I don't think he believed in the crystal ball. I think he was just trying to help the neighbor kid out.

I noticed Gomez hanging around a lot and began to worry about all the money in plain sight. Finally he flopped in the chair in front of me.

"I want another fortune," he said.

"What for?"

He gave his shoulders a sharp shrug. "I don't like the last one."

"Only one to a customer," I declared.

"Look in that glass ball again."

"Get wise, Gomez," I muttered, practically under my breath.

But he wasn't listening closely. "I been thinking about those bars on the windows," he said, his eyes looking down. "Maybe you made a mistake."

"Maybe. Maybe not."

"What if I step on the Tarantulas? We stop grabbing?"

"You mean, will that change your fortune?"

"Yeah. Change it. Look in the ball, amigo," he insisted.

He really believed there was something going on in this piece of glass. "You can't lie to the crystal," I said. "If you haven't gone straight—"

"Starting today," he mumbled.

I shrugged and nodded. "Cool. Your fortune's bound to be different. Let's check it out in a week and see."

He got up and left. I sat there, my head overheating. Looking at the faces of people passing by, I wondered how many still believed the world was flat. How about me?

"What are you staring at?" Daisy asked.

I found myself gazing hard into the crystal ball. "Giving it a final test," I said. I commanded it to come up with my mom's face. She could tell me herself if she were really gone. And did she really think I would become a writer?

"Well?" Daisy asked.

I just about gazed my eyes out of my head. But that confounded crystal stayed blank.

"The ball's a fake."

"I could have told you that, Pep."

On Saturday we all stood around watching as men began to raise an orange circus tent on the beach. It was only about the size of a barn and would hold a mere ninety-nine seats.

"Behold! The Venice-on-the-Beach Opera House," ex-Countess Liz Anne announced proudly, with a wave of her arm jangling with bracelets. "Our Metropolitan, my dears. Over the weekend we rehearse with a real orchestra. Today it's back to Main Street. Back to work, everyone!"

Holly was becoming nervous, which surprised me. She knew her part as if it were freshly etched inside her skull. What was there to get nervous about? Anyway, she forgot her script, which she clung to like a security blanket, and sent me home to get it.

So back I ran. And across from Casa de Sueños I saw a man in wide leather sandals with one foot resting on a boardwalk bench. He was looking at the house.

Not looking exactly. Scowling at it. Gazing as if he could see right through the sunny walls into the rooms. An alarm began to ring inside my head.

He was a man in a rumpled white suit.

STALKING THE STALKER

16

I froze. People flowed around me like ants around a stick. Was that the Toad standing there? Had he found us?

All I could see was one side of his face, but that was enough to raise the hair on my neck. He had a squashed, stepped-on nose and a jowly red cheek. He was mopping his neck with a white handkerchief. He wore a straw hat tipped forward on his head with a lot of light hair curling out under it. He had the scuffed, leathery look of someone fresh from cactus country. The Toad. The Horned Toad. It's him, I thought.

I backed off a little to make sure he didn't catch sight

of me. I could run for the police station down the boardwalk. But what if he took off? No, I wasn't going to let him out of my sight.

I'd follow him to his car. I'd get the license number.

But what if he turned out to be a dentist from New Orleans or something like that? I wiped the sweat off my forehead with the side of my arm. No, I told myself. Nobody went to the beach in a white suit. Not even tourists.

This was the Toad, all right. That's why he had his gaze clamped on Casa de Sueños. As I tightened my eyes, watching him, I wondered how he had tracked us down.

He glanced over my way once or twice, but I was just a face in the mob. He took off his hat and fanned himself. He waited.

And I waited.

He knew we lived there and must be figuring we'd show up. Who had tipped him off? I wondered if anyone besides Daisy at Casa de Sueños had seen that missing-kids flyer.

Then, hanging on to his scowl, he turned and started walking toward me. I faded off to one side until he passed. Would he have recognized me with my hair dyed blond? Maybe. Maybe not.

He was striding north along the boardwalk, eyes straight ahead, ignoring the fortune-tellers and T-shirt sellers and hot-grease hamburger joints.

He walked right past the Statue of Liberty without so much as a flickering glance. His mind was clearly elsewhere. On Holly, I thought. On me.

Then he turned right on Windward. I followed him past the neon-lit Tattoo Asylum and the dusty parked cars. He turned into the big white Marina Pacific Hotel. I watched him stride into the lobby as if he owned the place.

Gotcha! I thought. I'll tell the cops where to find you. You're history, Horned Toad. You'll be toast in handcuffs.

I backed off. I wished Holly were here to see this. It would make her day and her day and her day.

I ran past the Tattoo Asylum, the parked cars, and the souvenir joints. I crossed the boardwalk and hauled up at the police substation. It stood blocking the setting sun in a patch of beach grass. The front window looked like a theater box office. I rapped urgently on the glass.

Inside, a lady cop turned and gave me a smile through the window. I'd seen her around on the boardwalk. She had a beach tan and black eyelashes about a mile long. She looked more like a runner-up for Miss America than an officer of the law.

"Yes?"

"A man's been stalking us, and I found him!"

I blurted it out. If I looked wild-eyed and crazy, she was nice about it.

"That's serious," she said, as if to assure me that she wasn't taking me for some overexcited kid. She picked up a clipboard to begin making notes. "I'm Officer Gonzales. Your last name?"

I meant to answer fast—but answer what? Gomez? I felt a rising panic. You don't lie to a cop. But Holly would kill me if I spilled the beans, wouldn't she? Still, everything was changing. Now we were stalking the Toad.

"Kidd," I said. "My name's Kevin Michael Kidd."

I felt a huge relief to be myself again. Wouldn't Holly have done the same thing?

Officer Gonzales wrote down my name, and I let her have our address. I explained how the Toad had broken into our house in Albuquerque and stalked us all the way to Venice. No, I didn't know his name, "but I can lead you right to him!"

"Then we're standing in the wrong place," she said briskly. "Let's go."

She came out of a yellow side door and off we went.

She was in her beach uniform—dark blue shorts and a short-sleeved shirt. If she weren't wearing a pistol on her hip, you'd think she was off to a volleyball game. She was no taller than me, but she had a faster walk.

She turned a smile at everyone we passed, and somehow that gave me extra confidence in her. If the Toad gave her any trouble, she could whistle up a lot of help.

We strode up Windward, past the parked cars and the Tattoo Asylum. The small lobby of the Marina Pacific Hotel stood empty, except for a woman in a bathing suit helping herself to the help-yourself coffee. But I hadn't expected the Toad to be hanging around the lobby waiting for us.

"Hello, Miss Gonzales," the desk clerk said, throwing her a little salute.

"We're looking for a guest of yours," she declared. "Man in a white suit."

"Name?"

"Haven't a clue."

So I piped up. "Almost six foot tall. Wears sandals. Tanned face. Scowling eyes. He was just in here."

"Oh. That man in the white suit."

"Right," Officer Gonzales said.

"He came in to use the phone. He's not a guest of ours."

I looked at the unused phone on the wall. A weight was falling on me. "Is he still around somewhere?"

"Sorry, kid. A cab picked him up. A bird of passage. He's gone."

SHHH, A SECRET

17

I meandered back to Casa de Sueños, my shoulders folded in like an umbrella. What was I going to tell Holly? That the police would do a search for the Toad? That's what they'd said in Albuquerque.

If I told her the Toad was in Venice, I knew what she'd do. Lift her feet and run. We'd grab our stuff and flit out of here. He was too cunning for the cops.

But what about all that singing and coughing she was practicing? What about the opera? Her big chance would go down the drain. The show would collapse before it opened. And the ex-countess would brain her.

I saw Daisy hanging around the Statue of Liberty.

"Hello, Mrs. Niederhauser," I murmured. Her painted silver face didn't move a muscle.

Daisy came skipping along beside me as I continued on by. "How come you're not brushing off flies?" she asked.

"What are you talking about?"

"You look like the walking dead."

I stopped and drilled my eyes into hers. "Did you phone Albuquerque?"

"Why should I?"

"You know I'm that missing kid. Did you turn me in?"

"What missing kid?"

"The one in the mail."

"Was that you?" she asked.

We started walking again. "Of course it was."

"You didn't look kidnapped. You and your sister."

"We weren't. A creep was stalking us. That's why we were running away."

"No kidding?" She seemed to brighten at the idea, as if she envied the adventure.

"No kidding."

"I'll bet I know who turned you in."

I stopped and faced her again. "The potato-bug man?"

"Oh, he doesn't know anything that's going on."

"I noticed. Who, then?"

"Mr. Twinkletoes."

"What?"

"The tap dancer who moved out. Remember him?"

"He kept to himself," I said. "I hardly laid eyes on him."

"He said he didn't think your name was Gomez."

"It isn't."

"He called my mother the other day and asked if she still had that thing in the mail. He wanted to look at the pictures of those missing kids again."

"Yeah?"

"My mother said she never saw the thing. Looks like he found it somewhere else and decided to turn you in, huh?"

I took a deep breath. It must have been him. But what did it matter now?

A breeze had come up along the boardwalk and seemed to blow Holly into us. She had just come out of Casa de Sueños and was clutching her opera script with all ten of her red fingernails.

"Pep! Where have you been? You were going to get my score. Hello, Daisy."

I tried to give her a playful shrug. "You didn't say to hurry."

"Don't forget to eat dinner. You got money?"

"Buckets."

She rushed off, the wind at her back. I stared at her. A couple of girls on Rollerblades cut between us, like giggling ballet dancers wearing purple crash helmets. Crash helmets. Maybe Holly and I should wear crash helmets.

I felt a chill start down my spine. Holly needed to know that the Toad might be around the next corner. But tell her? And ruin Chickadee's brand-new career? There'd be no opening night for the opera. We'd be out of Venice like rockets.

Maybe the police would get the Toad behind bars. So keep your mouth shut, Pep. *Shhh.*

A VISIT FROM THE PAST

18

igns went up along the boardwalk announcing the opening performance of the Venice-on-the-Beach Opera Company. And if Holly's name wasn't in lights, Chickadee Gomez's was.

LA BOHÈME

Starring the exciting new soprano
Chickadee Gomez

The Toad had vanished. I kept checking with the police, but they hadn't spotted anyone in a white suit. Every time I approached Casa de Sueños, I stopped short to gaze around. And look behind me.

Where was he? Maybe he'd broken a leg, I thought. Or gotten sick. What if he changed into another suit? He'd slip right past the police. I was surprised he wasn't popping up in my dreams.

"What are you getting so nervous about?" Holly asked, doing stretching exercises along the boardwalk. "It's me that has to get up on the stage and enter, coughing. In Italian. Have you ever tried to cough in Italian?"

"Fine," I said. "And I'll get stage fright so you won't have to."

"Why would I get stage fright?"

"Doesn't everyone?"

"I know my part. I intend to float on stage as calmly as a swan."

"Sure." I didn't believe her. She was just trying to talk herself out of throwing up on opening night.

The first orchestra rehearsal came up on the weekend. The players were mostly volunteers from around town. The string section had two dentists and a psychiatrist in it. I was glad to know that if Holly got a toothache or went crazy on stage, help was right there in the orchestra pit.

"Splendid! Splendid!" ex-Countess Liz Anne

Wilber-Jones exclaimed as the musicians were putting away their instruments. "Ready for the footlights? The time is getting close! Men, tuxedos for opening night. Ladies, dresses long enough to trip over. Next week!"

By that time Miss Fiesta Foote was going to rehearsals. She had talked herself into a small part in the second act. She was going to play the toy seller. She gave the part so much bounce, you'd think she intended to stop the show.

When we got back to our room that night and turned on the light—Holly let out a big gasp.

I jumped out of my skin.

Our room was torn up. Clothing had been thrown everywhere. Someone had broken in.

Holly let out a half scream. "The Toad! He's found us!"

I looked at Holly and knew what she was going to say next. "Pack! We're out of here!" So I jumped in fast. I wasn't going to let the Toad trip up her career. He might be scaring us, but he wasn't shooting at us. Maybe I could start stalking *him*.

"I know who did this," I said calmly. "Gomez."

"Gomez? What are you talking about? You're Gomez!"

"There's another one. He runs a small gang on the boardwalk. The Tarantulas."

"What do we have he could want? Language tapes?"

I had to rack my head in a hurry. "He's just trying to scare me into joining up. I'll talk to him. I'll make him apologize, or I'll put the cops on him."

She was buying it. I was stretching the truth a mile wide, but she did calm down. Finally she began to put things away. I took a deep breath. The opera was still on. But what was the Toad searching for?

It was easy to find Gomez the next day. Daisy and I just set up the card table and the crystal ball, and before long there he was.

"Can you see movies in that thing?"

"Naw," I said. "There's no antenna."

"You see me in there again?"

"I just gave a look."

"What about them jailhouse bars?"

"They're fading a little. You must be doing something good."

"Yeah, amigo. I put the Tarantulas on hold."

"It's a start."

He pulled up his sunglasses. "Ain't that enough?"

"You need to do a good turn or two. You know where I live?"

"Yeah, I know."

"You know my sister. When she comes out of the house, just tell her you're sorry and walk away."

"Sorry for what?"

"Never mind. She'll understand."

"That's all I got to do? That'll square things with the crystal ball?"

"I was hoping you'd stake out our place for a few days. You and your ex-Tarantulas. If you see a man hanging around, a man in a white suit, make a lot of noise and follow him. He's on the ten-most-wanted list. All ten spots."

"Bad hombre, eh?" Then he leaned in closer. "Certain you can't get movies in that glass ball?"

"Not this model."

Once he'd wandered off, Daisy gave me a slight shake of her head. "He'll skin you alive when he realizes you're faking him."

A CUSTOMER FOR NOSTRADAMUS

19

The sea wind was blowing when the opera scenery came moving into the orange tent on the beach. Exactly ninety-nine folding seats were set out in front of the stage. The number of seats had something to do with union rules. More seats than that and the ex-countess would have to pay everybody.

We had canvas dressing rooms, one for the women, one for the men. All the singers seemed to walk around testing their vocal cords or nasal passages. The place sounded like a stockyard.

With the first dress rehearsal, seeing everyone in costume and the scenery in place, I changed my fix on the opera. It had gotten a paint job and looked kind of grand. Especially the second act, with Miss Fiesta pushing a cart full of toys through the Paris street while Daisy and I tagged along. The stage direction the ex-countess gave us was to behave like puppy dogs.

"Can either of you do a cartwheel?" she asked.

We both could, so we both did. She shook her golden head.

"Too much business. Just one of you."

I backed off and let Daisy do the business. As soon as she felt the stage under her feet, I could see a change come over her. It was as if she had found home base. Maybe she'd cartwheel herself someplace.

"And Chickadee, dear," the ex-countess said. "I'm going to ask you to make a great sacrifice. You must give up lipstick for the run of the show. Mimì, remember, is sick as a wombat. You are looking much too robust. She must look pale as death. Death with only the pilot light on. Got it? No lipstick."

Holly got a Kleenex and wiped her lips clean, and the rehearsal resumed. I found myself getting a little weepy at the end when Mimì, in the tenor's arms, coughs her last and the music rises like a tsunami and the curtain falls. It all made my scalp tingle. I didn't miss the electric guitars and bongo drums.

Holly slept in the next morning. She wanted to get some extra rest before Friday—opening night. Two days to go, and the clock was ticking away.

But I didn't have to rest my voice, so I borrowed the crystal ball again. Daisy helped me drag the stuff out to set up Nostradamus on the boardwalk. I had managed to pay Miss Fiesta almost a week's rent and was feeling proud of myself.

Daisy hung around for a while but wandered off with her drawing pad. Some dolphins were playing around offshore, and she wanted to sketch them. I called her back.

"Daisy, if you see a man in a white suit and sandals, draw him. The police are looking for the guy, but they don't know what he looks like."

"He from Albuquerque?" she asked.

I nodded. "The Toad. The stalker. In person."

She had already turned her back when someone sat down heavily to get his fortune read. He was wearing a big Hawaiian shirt that looked so new it might have still had its price tag on. He was wearing wide sandals and carrying a jacket over his shoulder. He began to wipe his neck with a handkerchief.

That jacket was white. My heart began to hammer.

I was looking into the eyes of the Toad.

MY BLOOD GETS ICY
20

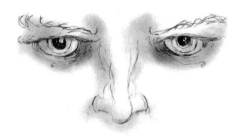

His eyes bored into mine like burning sticks. "Nostrrrrrradamus, eh? Eh, you expect me to believe you can see anything in that rrrrrrridiculous glass ball?"

"No, sir."

He rattled his *rrrrr*s, sounding like the tail of a diamondback about to strike. His voice had a kind of English accent, but heavily dipped into Bulgarian or Turkish or something thick and murky like that.

"Nevertheless," he said, his eyes still fixed on me, "nevertheless, you will amuse me, eh? You will tell me what you observe in the glass. Beasts, yes? Monsterrrrs, perhaps?"

I turned my head and gave Daisy a yell. Off in the sand she stopped and looked back at me, puzzled.

"Indeed," said the Toad. "Show me where the monsterrrrs are."

Monsters? Was he kidding? Or crazy?

But from the way he kept peering at me, it began to dawn on me that he wasn't fooled. He knew exactly who I was. The breath caught in my throat. My blood was running cold. I could feel sweat creep out all over my skin.

What was this weirdo doing now? Playing a game of cat and mouse with me?

I said. "Monsters? Any particular kind?"

"You tell me. Look hard, eh? Where you are hiding the beasts?"

I kept my eyes on the ball. What was he trying to tell me? That he'd been stalking us because he thought we had his monsters? Why wasn't he in a straitjacket?

Suddenly Daisy was at my elbow. "Pep?"

"You forgot something," I said. How could I tip her off to draw the man?

"What'd I forget?"

"What a memory! That greasy nose paint for your white skin. Oh, *suit* yourself. Get sunburned."

"What are you talking about?"

"Hang around."

I turned back to the Toad. "I don't think I can help you, sir."

He had wispy, sun-bleached eyebrows and gooseberry pale eyes. "Ah, but you can," he insisted with a deeply lined smirk.

I think Daisy began to catch on—the Toad's white pants, the white coat over his shoulder. Out of the corner of my eye I saw her turn over the pages of her sketchbook to a blank one.

The Toad leaned back, and something approaching a grin came over his lips. "Now I tell your fortune. You know what's good for you, your crystal ball will spill the beans, eh? It tells me where the monsterrrrs are, correct? Yes, positive! I'll be back."

With that he stood up and strode off into the passing crowd. He turned around once, to make sure I wasn't following him. Then he was off again.

My heart was still banging away. I turned to Daisy. "Did you get a good look at him?"

She was already beginning to sketch. "Pretty good."

"His shirt had flamingos all over it."

"I saw it."

"I'm going after him," I said. By now he was far enough off that he wouldn't realize he was being tailed. But by the time I reached the corner, he was gone. Ducked in somewhere. I looked all around, but that Hawaiian shirt had vanished. I guessed he knew I would try to follow him.

I gave it up after a while, feeling outwitted and stupid, and returned to Daisy and her drawing. By that time the Toad's face was coming up on the page like a photograph developing. "His nose is shorter," I said. "It looked stepped-on."

"I'll shorten it."

Daisy was good. Very good.

"Nostradamus?" exclaimed a familiar voice. "Kevin! What in Sam Hill are you doing?"

It was Holly, and her temper was flaring red. She didn't know that she had come within minutes of bumping into the Toad. It was hard not to blurt it out, but I managed to keep my jaws shut. I hoped Daisy wouldn't spill the beans.

I lifted my arms and talked fast. "This crystal ball has paid us a week's rent," I said.

"I know. Fiesta told me. What do you know about telling fortunes?"

"I read a book about it."

"Nostradamus, Junior! What delusions of grandeur! What a crock of nonsense!"

"I'm passing out nothing but good news," I said.

She was so wired, it was a wonder her hair wasn't standing on end. "Don't you realize what you're doing? What if you make a few lucky guesses?"

"Then good for Nostradamus, Junior."

"You think so? What if they come true?"

"It's harmless, Holly," I said.

"Is it? People will think there really is something to that crystal ball stuff when you get something right. You'll make believers out of them."

"Oh."

"Yes, oh. You're going to give the money back."

She was trying to sound like my mom. And she was coming close. "How am I supposed to run after a bunch of strangers? Anyway, it was giggle money, Holly. Nobody gave us much."

"You'll give it to charity," she said.

"How am I going to do that? I'll have to tell fortunes to raise the cash."

She'd get the money, she said, and stalked off. I shook my fingers as if I had burned them. I guess I had.

Holly had just put me out of the fortune-telling business.

Daisy didn't quite finish the drawing, but it was close enough. I asked her to print across the bottom that people were to notify the police.

I stopped at the copy shop and then ran the artwork over to the police station. Officer Gonzales was on duty and recognized me with a smile.

"How you doing, Pep?"

"Here's the stalker!"

She tightened her eyes on Daisy's drawing. "Great! This'll help. He looks like a vulture with a bad nose job."

Later, Daisy and I tacked up copies along the boardwalk. She was all smiles. For her, it must have been like having a one-woman art show.

Along came Gomez. "I'm clean," he said, flashing his teeth in a lopsided grin. "Wanna have another look in your magic ball, amigo?"

"I already checked you out," I said. "You're so clean you could do detergent commercials."

"No kidding."

"The gray bars are gone. Vanished. Poof!"

"Gomez," he said, "if I'm going to level out, how do I get a job? I ain't never worn square-toe shoes before."

"You know the big guy who juggles watermelons?"

"Yeah."

"He's still looking for a hat man. It's an entry-level job, but you could end up president of the United States. I'd vote for you."

"Yeah?"

"Us Gomezes have to stick together, no?"

"Sí. What's a hat man?"

"I'll explain later."

He looked up from the picture of the Toad. "That the bad guy? The white suit? He bumped into me an hour ago."

"Next time, follow him, amigo," I said.

THE WILTED LOTUS

21

Maybe the Toad saw his picture hanging around and was keeping himself out of sight. The beach flypaper was stuck with people, and a sea breeze was shaking and rustling the spiky green tops of the palms.

"Those trees are having a bad hair day," Holly said.

She was looking out the window. Flags were snapping over the opera tent, and we could see people buying tickets at the box office. It was Friday. The curtain would be rising at eight o'clock.

Three hours.

Holly tried some yoga out of a library book, to calm

her nerves. She folded her legs in the lotus position. I ambled on downstairs.

The ground floor was deserted. Even Daisy was having her hair done for opening night. Only two hours to go, for the ex-countess insisted that the company—us— be there an hour early.

Holly said she wouldn't be able to eat until after the opera, but there were no butterflies in my stomach. The boardwalk smelled of hamburgers. I bought one to walk around with and ended up at the tent. Miss Fiesta must have volunteered to sell tickets, because that's what she was doing.

"We're going to sell out!" she announced when she saw me. "For the whole weekend, looks like!"

I was kind of amazed. This wasn't a nickels-and-dimes show. Adult tickets were thirty dollars. With two shows tomorrow and a Sunday matinee, ex-Countess Liz Anne Wilber-Jones might be able to pay everyone.

I wandered around inside the tent and tried out one of the seats. Imagine paying that much money to sit in a folding chair and listen to a lot of fancy screaming. I would have guessed the opera wouldn't draw flies. But I was beginning to understand it, too.

We'd better be good, I told myself. And if Holly

threw up on stage, not to worry. I'd heard her practice so much, I'd step right in and sing the part myself, except for the high notes.

The musicians were beginning to arrive and set up. The minutes were ticking away.

As I left, Miss Fiesta said, "Break a leg."

"What?"

"That's showbiz talk. It means good luck."

I grinned back. "Break a leg."

When I got back to the room, Holly was no longer sitting in the yoga position. The lotus had wilted. She was flat on the floor. A scarf was tied around her mouth to gag her from waking the neighbors. With his back to the window, a small gun in his hand, sat the Toad.

"Waiting for you, young Nostradamus," he said, rolling his *rrrrr*s.

THE HUNCHBACK OF
NOTRE DAME

22

The Toad lowered his chin and fixed me with his pale gooseberry eyes. "We will lay our cards on the table, yes? This foolish young lady is being very stubborn. So. Where is the map, please? It was not left behind in Albuquerque. So you must have it with you. Not so? Correct?"

"What map?" I mumbled.

He made a sizzling sound with his lips. "Again you ask, like your sister, what map? We will sit here until your memories are refreshed, eh?"

Holly began making urgent sounds through the gag around her mouth. I said, "We've got to get out of here.

The opera show is about to start!"

"No one will be leaving these walls."

"But Holly's the star! She's playing the lead!"

"She has my congratulations."

"They can't lift the curtain without her!"

"Is there not an understudy?"

"No," I replied.

"That is too bad."

"We don't know anything about your map or your monsters!" I shouted.

"Keep your voice down," he warned, giving the gun a small wave to draw attention to it.

Beside his shoulder, through the open window, I could see the opera tent. I was able to spot members of the company arriving. I saw ex-Countess Liz Anne Wilber-Jones in a silver dress that gave off lights like a Fourth of July sparkler. She'd soon be wondering why Holly hadn't turned up.

With her hands behind her back, Holly was writhing about, desperate to break loose.

"Sir," I said, beginning to doubt that you could reason with a man with bugs in his head, "do you think we wouldn't tell you about your map and your monsters if we knew anything? Don't ruin the opera, please. Let us go."

"Ah, aha! But you do know." He fished a pink letter out of his coat pocket and waved it in the air. "It's here, in this letter. Confirmed."

I almost recognized the envelope. Pink. My mother wrote on pink stationery.

"Is that one of the letters you stole from our house?"

"Let's just say it came into my possession."

Anger flared up inside me. You rattlesnake, I thought! You mangy creep. How dare you take one of Mom's letters! It belongs to me. Holly and me.

I looked around for something to bang him over the head with. All that caught my eye was the framed movie poster of *The Hunchback of Notre Dame* on the wall. If only that monster would come to life!

I managed to keep my voice steady. "We'd like our letters back."

"Not possible. So we shall sit here quietly until you children realize it is useless to continue this deceit. Yes? Where did your mother hide the map?"

"You knew her?" I asked.

"We were occasional colleagues."

I hesitated, but then said flat out, "She's not dead, is she?"

"But of course."

I found myself holding my breath. "But of course, what?"

"The earthquake. She didn't survive."

"How do you know?"

"I was there," he replied almost airily. "As I told you, we were jealous colleagues."

"You said occasional."

"Occasional and jealous."

I gave him a new look. "Is your name Kickshaw?"

"Perhaps," he answered, grinning suddenly.

"My mother had to order you off the dig. She wrote us about you in several letters. Kickshaw. That's who you are."

He gave his head a little dip. "Ah. Is a name soon to be famous."

Is that what he was doing? Waiting for his close-up? "You escaped the earthquake?"

"With a few pesky bruises."

"But you saw my mother—"

"From across the valley. Clearly. I watched through glasses as she entered the cave."

"You were spying on her?"

"But of course. And that nervous mountain is now her tombstone. A noble tombstone any archaeologist would be proud to rest under, eh? So the map will be of no further use to her. To me, yes. She is quite, quite dead."

I glared at him as his news fit inside my head once and for all. No more dreaming about gentleman bandits and ransom notes and amnesia. I looked over at Holly. She had heard. But she had known all along. Mom was quite, quite dead.

The still-bright sun had lowered itself to the window. The Toad—Kickshaw—was transformed into a bulky silhouette. I watched over his shoulder as theatergoers were drawn into the tent below. It sat there aglow like a pumpkin in the sun.

"There are going to be people banging at the door any minute, looking for Holly," I said. "Sir. Let her out of here."

"That would be stupid of me, would it not, eh? Until you tell me about the beasts and the map, the theater curtain will remain down. If anyone comes knocking, you will remain silent as a mouse. Yes?"

I said, "A map to what? Something my mother dug up? Coronado's golden armor?"

He made a dismissive sound with his breath, like a bicycle tire going flat. "Such a trifle, that. And truth to tell, it is already in my possession."

"It was you who stole it?"

He ignored my question as if it were too obvious to need an answer. "It is the big fish I am after. The whale in your mother's murky sea of field notes—one of the golden cities of Cíbola. Ha! You know why the conquistadors couldn't find those treasured streets, eh, four hundred years ago?"

"My mother didn't believe that stuff!"

"Didn't she? That was only to pull the wool over us, yes? She had followed the footsteps of those fools in their rusting armor! Rumors lured them north, into Oklahoma, eh? And Kansas. Misguided idiots! They dragged along great empty wagons to haul off the tons of plunder. Even the great Hernando de Soto got the Cíbola fever. Yes, yes, he abandoned his preposterous fountain of youth in Florida to rush west toward the golden cities. But it was your mother who stubbed her boot on one of those bejeweled cities. Where?"

He let the question float in the air.

"In Mexico!" he declared.

I could see that Holly had stopped writhing and struggling. This was fresh news, and she was caught up by it, too. Mom had found one of the lost cities? A gasp caught in my throat.

Kickshaw huffed out a dispirited sigh. "But where exactly in Mexico had she stubbed her boot?" he asked. "Such a big country. But we know your clever mother made a map, eh? Yes?"

He pulled out and waved the pink envelope again. "It's written here, in so many words. Yes, inducing me to return to your house in Albuquerque. Demanding that I search the walls, the ceiling, even the cement floor of the garage. Every square inch. But do I have the map? Alas. No."

"What words?" I asked. "Exactly what did my mom say?"

He unfolded the letter, found the place, and pretended to read, but I could see that he knew my mother's words by heart. " 'When I was home three weeks ago, I jotted down a dig location that I wish to keep quite secret for the moment. You'll find it in Kevin's wild things. Do keep it safe for me.' "

He refolded the letter sharply. "Now you will tell me which of your old wild beasts and monsters? Which of your childish stuffed toys, please? It is not in this room. Where have you hidden it, eh? For I intend to march into the history books as the discoverer of the first fabled city of Cíbola! I shall be famous, you see."

It was hard not to burst out laughing. He had missed it! Mom had said flat out where she had jotted down the map, but he had missed it. Stuffed monsters? He had pulled the wool over his own eyes.

At that moment there came a knock and a voice at the door. Kickshaw put the gun to his lips like a finger, warning us to keep our mouths shut.

"Hey, Gomez! You in there?" It was Bumpy Rhoades. "Curtain's going up in ten minutes. Where are you?"

He knocked again, harder, rattling the framed movie poster on the wall. Then he left.

My eyes met the Hunchback of Notre Dame's. A crazy idea came over me, and I didn't have time to think twice about it.

"I know where the map is!" I announced. The words were just out of my mouth when I dropped one shoulder like the hunchback, twisted my mouth—and froze.

I stood there like a mannequin. Stiff as the Statue of Liberty. I stopped blinking. I almost stopped breathing.

He'd have to think I was having a strange fit or something. And just when I was about to give him the big secret of the map, the way actors were always doing in the movies.

He'd have to get up from the chair and cross over to me, and he'd probably try to shake the answer out of me. I'd try to catch him by surprise, burst back to life, and knock the gun out of his hand.

But Holly had a better idea. The moment Kickshaw walked over to me, she began rolling herself on the floor behind him. All I'd have to do is push.

My eyes stared off at the hunchback on the wall. They began to tear. But if it killed me, I wasn't going to blink.

"What is this craziness?" he sputtered. "So! Where do you have the map! Speak!"

I just stood there, like the hunchback himself.

He did begin to shake me by the shoulders. My muscles tensed all over. We were interrupted by another banging at the door. I heard Miss Fiesta's voice. "Did you faint in there? We're holding the curtain!"

She didn't wait for an answer. She pushed open the door. When she saw Holly on the floor, she let out a scream that must have startled the seagulls outside the window.

I chose that moment to spring back to life. I blinked my eyes and shoved Kickshaw backward. He tripped over Holly and hit the floor.

"He's got a gun!" I yelled out.

Miss Fiesta kicked off a shoe and hit his wrist with the stiletto heel. "Not anymore," she called out as the gun skittered over toward the window.

I skittered after it. Miss Fiesta was even faster. She had the gun in the Toad's face before he got to his knees.

He raised his hands and straightened up. He gave me a hard sneer. Now that I had admitted I knew where to find the map, he was telling me to beware of shadows. He'd be in one. Then he fled without a sound. Quick as lightning.

"We've got to call the cops!" I shouted to Miss Fiesta. She was already untying Holly.

"Plenty of time for that! We're all due onstage! Help me. The countess is having fits!"

SHOWTIME

23

The curtain went up fourteen minutes late. The house was sold out. Miss Fiesta said there were a couple of important people out there, but she didn't say who they were.

The men singers went into action the moment the curtain cleared. They were supposed to be in Paris, but they began to joke around in Italian. They were practically freezing to death in the attic room. One of them was a painter and another a poet-playwright. He tossed his new play into the fireplace to warm the room.

All this gave Holly time to get into costume and warm up her throat. Everyone was fussing around her, fixing a lace collar on her dress and monkeying around with her hair. Meanwhile she was making sounds like a sick cow.

"Lovely, lovely!" exclaimed ex-Countess Liz Anne Wilber-Jones in a state of desperation. "The candle! The candle! Mimì enters with a candle in her hand. No! Don't light it. Her candle has gone out and she's going next door to beg a light from Rodolfo. Was no one paying attention during rehearsals?"

With all this static in the air, Holly spoke up. Calmly. It didn't look like she was going to throw up, after all.

"Countess," she said. "At the end of the last act I would like you to make an announcement. Say that Chickadee Gomez was unable to appear in tonight's production. At the last minute the role of Mimì was sung by the soprano from Albuquerque, Holly Kidd."

"Who on earth is Holly Kidd?"

"I am."

"What are you talking about?"

"I don't have to hide any longer."

"You must tell me all about it—later! Get onstage. Your cue is coming up!"

She adjusted the angle of the candle in Holly's hand

and gave her a gentle shove toward the stage.

I stood there, dazed for a moment. Did Holly mean I wasn't Pep Gomez any longer? I'd have to be Kevin Kidd again? Well, okay. But I'd never forget Gomez. He had been like one of those henna tattoos on the board-walk. He wasn't going to wash right off.

I didn't go on until the second act, so I had time to change into my costume. From the dressing room I heard Holly singing her heart out onstage.

There was a lot of applause when the act ended. Holly came offstage kind of floating in midair. She had breezed through her debut. She wasn't even sweating.

But I was. When we were set for the street scene, as the second-act curtain was about to rise, I felt a touch of stage fright. I think I would have forgotten my lines, if I'd had any.

The moment the lights hit us, Daisy did her cart-wheel around Miss Fiesta and the toy cart. Then she gave the audience a flash of her straightened white teeth. They were blinding.

As a spear-carrier, I gave my all to the part. I strut-ted around the toy cart as if I were going to buy every-thing. I hardly had time to worry about the Toad. Now that I knew his name—Kickshaw—the police would have an easier time putting manacles on him. I'd head for the substation the moment the opera finished.

Daisy did another cartwheel, and the toy cart led us offstage into the wings. I wiped my forehead and flung the sweat off my fingers. I gave Daisy a smile. She laughed back. We had survived our debut.

The opera ended to such a burst of applause and cheering you'd think it had been a soccer victory. Ex-Countess Liz Anne Wilber-Jones came out in her sparkling silver dress and her gold-spun hair, and held up her hand to quiet the crowd.

When she announced that a last-minute substitute had sung the role of Mimì, those operagoers went wild. Miss Fiesta counted aloud backstage every time Holly had to go out front for a bow. Holly got eleven curtain calls.

In the dressing room the ex-countess introduced Holly to a few of her friends. They were going to get up a scholarship to send Holly to a big-time school of music in New York. We'd be heading east!

We walked home, all of us together. Bumpy Rhoades was actually wearing a rented tuxedo, and the Statue of Liberty had gotten all dressed up in a shiny green dress. She was talking and giggling plenty. I guess she stored up tons of funny conversation between Shakespeare's plays when she was doing her silent boardwalk act. She said Holly had made that uppity tenor playing Rodolfo look like he was merely gargling.

With Casa de Sueños practically in front of us, I saw Gomez there waiting for me against the wall. I pulled Holly aside.

"I'm going to the police to say the Toad had us at gunpoint. That ought to add a few years to his jail time."

"Okay."

"And I'll tell them your car was stolen."

"Why bother? It was mostly junk."

"But I had some old books in the car. Remember?"

"I'm sorry about that, Kevin."

"One of them has Mom's map written in it. Remember the first book I ever learned to read? And used to read over and over."

"The Sendak book?"

"That's what the Toad was talking about, but he didn't know it. Sure, monsters. Sure, beasts. It was *Where the Wild Things Are.* Mom must have used it to write in. To write down the map."

She stopped to face me. "It was in the car? When it was stolen?"

I nodded. "Mom figured I wouldn't part with it."

"You remember the license number of the car?"

"Of course. See ya."

She went on in with the others. I went over to Gomez.

"I get some brownie points?" he asked.

"For what?"

"The hombre you want to step on. I followed him outta here."

"You saw him?"

"Yeah," said Gomez, smiling wide. "All red in the face like he was eating raw chilies."

"Where'd he go?"

"To his hotel. Up the beach."

"You're a genius, Gomez."

"I know."

"Let's go."

"Where?"

"The police. Come on."

"They give out brownie points?"

DUST THE STREETS
WITH GOLD

24

L ike a bloodhound leading the way, Gomez, the real Gomez, led the police and me to a yellow merry-go-round building on the Santa Monica pier. There were rooms above it, and Kickshaw had rented one.

He must have seen the police coming, for he was off like a roadrunner. He got in with the merry-go-round horses, but they weren't going anywhere but in circles. It sounded like someone cracking walnuts when the cops slapped handcuffs on him.

I got a last look at the Toad behind bars. The police interviewed everybody, including Miss Fiesta, who still had his gun. That would be evidence.

"Maybe we'll locate your stolen car, but don't hold your breath," said Officer Gonzales softly. "It's been awhile. By now that VW could be anywhere between Seattle and Tierra del Fuego."

"It's a book we need to get back," I said.

"People who steal cars don't read books," she said simply.

"It's pretty beat up," I answered. "I read it a zillion times."

"You can start calling the used bookstores. But the car thief probably dumped your book somewhere. Good luck."

Holly had two performances on Saturday and Sunday. She wasn't exactly focused on finding the lost cities of Cíbola. But I got on the phone and called around for a copy of *Where the Wild Things Are*. An old copy with my name written in the upper right-hand corner of the first page. Any luck? No luck.

When Holly saw me hanging a frown on my face, she said, "What does it matter if those cities of gold remain undiscovered for another four hundred years? And how come Mom was keeping it a secret?"

"Search me."

"You know Mom no more believed in those golden cities than she did sea serpents and mermaids. Maybe she just intended to put that greedy toad Kickshaw on. She wrote how he'd been spying on her."

"Yeah," I said with a sharp nod.

"Mom had a sense of humor, and it would serve him right. He was as anxious to be deluded as those people who stopped at your crystal ball to get their fortunes told."

"But what if the map is real?"

"A map to what? Maybe what she found were some four-hundred-year-old Zuñi mud huts. We won't know unless *Where the Wild Things Are* turns up."

The book could be floating around anywhere between Seattle and Tierra del Fuego. That was a dismal thought.

Holly was still talking. "You really want to find the cities of Cíbola? Look around, Kevin. How about Venice? See those crowds on the boardwalk? And remember what Bumpy said?"

"The wannabes? Everyone looking for a movie close-up."

"And some will get it and end up driving a Mercedes. Look at the parking lots. Herds of

Mercedeses and BMWs and even a few Jaguars. The streets of Venice are paved with gold."

"Okay, okay," I said. "But I'm going to hang in there and keep checking the bookstores."

With the Toad no longer stalking us, Holly phoned the bank in Albuquerque and had them transfer her account to Venice. Almost the first thing she did was write out $250 to some charities. I promised never to gaze into a crystal ball again.

The opera would be running every weekend until the end of summer. We flew to Albuquerque to see how the Toad had trashed our house, and put it up for sale. We hung around only long enough to say good-bye to a few friends. The way we had disappeared, they figured we must have been abducted by extraterrestrials.

On the plane back I thought, Hello, Venice, good-bye Albuquerque. I'd be glad to see Daisy and Gomez again. Bumpy Rhoades said Gomez was turning into a star hat man.

"Guess what?" Daisy asked.

"You're going to take acting lessons."

"How did you know?"

"And you'll get a letter in the mail, and fortune will smile on you."

"Oh, that old stuff," she said. "My lessons. A lucky guess, huh?"

"The moment I saw the spotlight hit you on opening night, I knew you were doomed for acting lessons."

As the weeks went by, I hardly bothered phoning bookstores anymore. There were a number of used copies of *Where the Wild Things Are* around, but none with my name in the upper right-hand corner. Maybe, in years to come, somebody would gaze into the right copy and wonder what Mom's little green handwriting was all about. Maybe me. Maybe not.

The opera had its last performance over the Labor Day weekend. By that time Holly and I were pretty well packed for our trip east. We were going to live in Manhattan while the experts at the music academy buffed up her voice with diamond polish. I didn't need a crystal ball to figure out that school would be starting and that's where I'd be.

But we were still at Casa de Sueños when T. Tex Rimbo, the potato-bug guy, honked the horn of a brand-new Italian foreign car parked at the curb. It was a metallic gold. The low-slung hood looked like the engine had enough horsepower to fly to the moon.

"Jump in, everyone!"

"You win the lottery?" Miss Fiesta asked.

"Nothing so common, darling. Giant potato bugs are poised to take over the world. I sold my screenplay, sweethearts!"

I guessed Holly was right. The streets of Venice were sprinkled with the same fairy dust that had lured the conquistadors into cactus country. There sat T. Tex Rimbo looking like old Don Francisco Coronado himself, all decked out in his flashing golden armor.

We used the occasion to say a lot of good-byes. Bumpy Rhoades drove us to the airport a few miles down the coast. He went inside with us.

Before turning to go, he pulled a surprise out of his sleeve. "I'll be doing my medical internship in Brooklyn. Across the river from you. See ya."

"See ya!" I exclaimed.

Our plane swung out over the ocean. For a few moments it gave us orchestra seats for a view of Venice below. I could pick out Casa de Sueños with the prairie fire of red flowers across its roof.

I gave Daisy and Gomez an extra little wave. I'd predicted she'd receive a letter. I'd write her one from New York. Straight ahead.

Hello and good-bye, I thought.

AUTHOR'S NOTE

Novels are not created out of thin air, but this one came close. It began with nothing more than a passing glance at a street performer in Honolulu. A woman stood motionless, gowned in silver as the Statue of Liberty. I wondered how she could keep her right arm raised all evening long. Only after I paused for a second glance did I catch on. But how, too, could the mannequin acts keep from blinking their eyes?

Wheels began to spin in my head. I wondered if there might be a novel in these street performers.

We have boardwalk entertainers in Venice, California, a few miles from where I live. I began hanging around the beach, taking notes.

I started the novel with no plot in mind. I hoped that I'd find one before I reached the end.

When the great English actress Judi Dench steps onstage, she calls it "going out on the ice." Writers, especially those of us who prefer to improvise our stories as we go along, also are accustomed to ice underfoot. I slip a lot.

But the risks are worth it for me: Inspirations of the moment pop up. The fortune-telling scenes in these pages grew out of a flashback to my teenage years when a friend read my palm. "Sid," he announced darkly, "you have a short lifeline." I knew that meant, according to the lore, that I would have a short life.

Now, I also knew that fortune-telling—palmistry, tea-leaf reading, crystal gazing, tarot card reading, studying the entrails of chickens, all of it—was ancient and absurd numskullery. Nevertheless, that prophecy of impending doom haunted me for twenty years. Had I had the money, I might have gone to a surgeon and had my lifeline lengthened.

Sheer accident, too, helps me keep my balance on the ice. It was pure chance that I stumbled across the sort of detail that formal histories sweep under the carpet. One of the Spanish conquistadors, Coronado, rattled around the early Southwest wearing show-off, blazing golden armor. And that led me to the Seven Cities of Cíbola. Just what I needed! Thank you, Don Francisco.

I have never lost a novel because I could not figure out the ending. But this one almost turned to ashes as I found myself nearing the last chapters. I couldn't figure out a dramatic scene to wrap things up—until the very last instant. Suddenly there it was. Like a jack-in-the-box.

To return to my unpromising lifeline. It's still brief. Despite the lore, as I skate on the ice, I have reached the serene age of 112.

Sid Fleischman
Santa Monica, California